OOZE

Here to Nowhere

David Brown

PARKWAY PRESS™

#1 Independent Publisher™
P.O. Box 252
Niles, OH 44446-0252
United States
www.ParkwayPress.com

ISBN-10: 0982808976
ISBN-13: 9780982808979
Printed in the United States of America
OOZE
HERE TO NOWHERE
FIRST EDITON

Front Cover Design by David L. Brown
Interior Design by Jera Publishing, LLC
"The End" Artwork by Brandon A. Brown

<u>Parental Advisory</u>: This novel contains adult content. It is not suitable for young children.

Acknowledgments

To Alýssa and Brandon: I love you with all my heart. Thank you for being such wonderful kids! Special thank you to my late father, Jimmy Brown. I miss you more than you know. Thank you also to my mother, Doris Brown, my late sister, Buena Fleck, and my remaining family.

Edited by Geri Clark. Also edited by AutoCrit and EditMinion (Manuscript Editing Software Programs).

Also written by David Brown

Geek 'n Dork
Amazing

OOZE

1

THE DOCTOR'S WAITING ROOM was small and cramped.

Neopolitina, better known as Neo, was hardly impressed. The ugly off-white colored walls, lined with cheap plastic chairs, only added to her sudden sense of claustrophobia. At the far end of the room, a bored-looking receptionist tapped at a keyboard with a single, neatly manicured finger. Her jaw worked a piece of gum; it appeared occasionally between the young woman's lips as purple bubble before popping noisily and disappearing again.

An elderly man and a twenty-something man sat waiting for their turn to see the doctor. The younger man's face was buried in his cell phone, his thumbs flying over the tiny keyboard, while the older man flipped through the pages of a magazine, pausing now and again to raise a hand to his mouth to cover a dry, hoarse, cough.

Neo glanced at the magazine in the man's hands: *Food & Wine,* the title read.

Why do doctor's offices always have such weird tastes in magazines? She wondered, as she made her way over to the receptionist's desk. Is it due to some obscure magazine subscription especially designed for doctors', dentists', and hospital waiting rooms?

The receptionist was so engrossed with whatever she was doing on with her computer, that she didn't even notice Neo patiently waited for a response in front of her desk. Almost five foot ten, with a shock of curly, dark brown hair and pale blue eyes, Neo cleared her throat loudly after a half minute of standing there with not even a glance from the young woman.

"Hi, I'm Neo Kao from the *Times*. I have a ten o'clock appointment with Doctor Williams," she announced.

The receptionist, momentarily halting her constant chewing so she could push the gum to the other cheek, glanced up from her laptop, which Neo could now see had a YouTube music video showing.

"I'm sorry," the woman said, "I didn't quite hear your name. What did you say it was?" The bubblegum put in another brief appearance, flashing a glimpse of purple against her white teeth.

"Neo...Kao," the reporter repeated slowly, just to make sure the receptionist heard it correctly. "I'm from the *Los Angeles Times* to interview Doctor Williams about the clinical trial he's working on."

The receptionist made an obvious pretense of checking her laptop before picking up the phone sitting on her desk and fingering a pair of numbers.

"Doctor Williams, I have a Nayapolitano Kao here to see you. Yes, she *says* she's a reporter...okay, thank you, doctor."

Neo matched the woman's sarcastic smile at the obvious *mangling* of her name. "His office is just down the hallway," the receptionist continued, gesturing toward a hallway behind her desk. "Third door on the left."

"Thanks," Neo said as she walked in the direction the woman had indicated, but the receptionist's attention had already returned back to the pressing issues of her laptop music video.

"Rachet ho," Neo whispered under her breath on the way down the hallway before she knocked on the office door.

An hour later, Neo closed the doctor's office door behind her. She let out a small sigh of relief as the sounds and smells of Los Angeles rolled over her from a nearby open window just off the hallway. She loved LA. She had grown up in Big Timber, Montana, a small farm town that was as indistinguishable as the numerous other towns surrounding it. Looking back, it seemed like she had spent most of her younger years just waiting for the moment when she could get out of town and move somewhere, anywhere where there were people – a lot of people.

Neo had never *meant* to be a reporter. She had fallen into it by sheer luck rather than a planned design. Like many small towns, hers had an even smaller local paper. It published an issue once a week covering everything from the local police arrest record to the usual small-town happenings. The paper had been looking for an entry-level reporter to cover the local town board meetings, and Neo had, as an afterthought, decided to apply for the position after graduating from high school.

Robert, the editor, had interviewed her. He was a heavily bearded, grizzly old man who looked seventy but could well have been one hundred for all she could tell. He had been in the newspaper business since the Second World War when he had served in the U.S. Army. He had told her that he would give her a chance and pay her as a part-time news researcher for a few weeks.

"If you can hack it, we'll see about it becoming permanent," he had told her.

Neo put every ounce of energy she had into the job in a way that she never imagined possible. Within a month, she had secured the title of staff writer for the small paper. One year later, she found herself promoted to lead writer.

"Girly, you seem as comfortable as a flea on a dog's ass," Robert had eloquently described her success. She worked at the tiny paper for another four years before she felt she had enough experience to apply for work as a reporter at a much larger newspaper.

She had been pleasantly surprised by the number of requests for interviews she received, even though she had no formal college education. The interest in her skills and talents built up her confidence. She finally decided to accept an offer from the *Los Angeles Times*. It was too good to pass up, and served as her ticket out of Big Timber.

***

Neo, twenty-seven, had been working the metro desk at the *Los Angeles Times* for five years and she loved every minute of it. She knew the job would never make her a glamorous millionaire, but it paid the bills. She never worried about where the next paycheck was coming from. She lived alone and didn't have a lot of overhead that other longer-tenured journalists had, such as taking care of a family.

She hated driving to work every day in the congested Los Angeles traffic. She instead sold her late model Ford

Mustang two years ago and opted for a bicycle. She could be anywhere she needed to be in less than ten minutes.

She figured riding a bike would allow her to do her part to save the environment from pollutants, spend less time stuck in traffic jams, and she could save the money she would have spent paying a ridiculously amount for a gallon of gas at the pumps. For longer trips, she would usually take a cab or take advantage of the city's metro public transportation bus services.

No matter how much she loved the job and the city, there would always be days like this early-August 2013, day. It was smoldering hot, close to one-hundred degrees with seventy-five percent humidity. When you coupled the nausea-inducing humidity and heat with the gum-chewing receptionist and the equally annoying doctor from earlier, you had the makings of a less than perfect day. Yet, Neo didn't mind. It was almost noon and she had her first story for the day sewed up, which meant she was already ahead of schedule.

She had the choice to either head back to the newsroom or grab a bite to eat at a local café where should could then write up her news article. She pulled her cell phone from her pocket and checked her itinerary for the day. She had two hours to kill until her next appointment.

There was a small internet café a block away that she knew served up a scrumptious egg-salad sandwich. Thinking about it made her stomach grumble. She unlocked the chain securing her bike to a no-parking sign, slung her backpack over her shoulder, and headed in the direction of lunch.

***

Neo pedaled her bike to a slow roll in front of the café. She hopped off and chained it to the security rack at the side of the entrance way, and strolled inside the eatery. As she entered the air-conditioned interior, she felt the sweat under her armpits chill, giving her an uncomfortable shiver. The upbeat sound of a top-forty song playing over the speakers and the smell of roasted coffee and fresh baked bread immediately grabbed her attention, causing her stomach to grumble again in anticipation.

A warm, honest smile from the café's owner greeted Neo as she walked to the counter.

"Good afternoon, my dear. What can I get for you today?" the man asked in a slight accent displaying his Greek ancestry.

"I'll take one of your delicious Cinnamon Dolce Lattes," she said after browsing the chalkboard list of coffees, "and an egg-salad sandwich on wheat bread for here, please."

The café was fairly empty. The lunchtime rush was still an hour or so away. She had her selection of tables and chose a four-seater near the window where she could keep an eye on her bike while she ate. She pulled her laptop from the backpack, powered it up, and synced it with the café's wireless Internet signal.

She clicked on her email icon and waited for it to load any emails she might have received since the interview with the grumpy old doctor earlier. There was a message from her editor at the *Times* reminding her to get her article in before deadline, along with the usual collection of unwanted spam promising to increase her breast size and offering cheap prescription medication imported directly from Japan. Nothing much important.

She checked NBC news on her web browser. There was the usual potpourri of stories on the news website's front page such as conflicts still raged across some God-forsaken third-world country, a politician had been caught in a lie *again*, reports of some strange weather throughout Europe, and some depressing stock market numbers that meant her 401(k) was going to be worth less than it was yesterday. She clicked on the weather article and began reading.

The Associate Press was reporting a strange phenomenon all throughout Europe, the online article said. Local government agencies were reporting "an unknown yellow-red precipitation" with no apparent meteorological cause. The first case had been reported in Berlin, Germany, over ten-hours ago. Similar reports of what the news agency had conveniently, if somewhat awkwardly, labeled *"ooze rain"* were coming in from Poland, Finland, Netherlands, Russia, the UK, and France as the day had gone by.

"Anything interesting going on in this crazy world of ours?" the café owner asked as he placed the plate with her sandwich next to her latte.

Neo raised her head from her laptop screen and smiled. "Not unless you want to talk about the weather," she said. She took a large bite from her sandwich, and being careful not to let any crumbs fall on her keyboard, she continued reading the online news report.

NBC had decided to avoid the European press's "ooze rain" description. Her reporter's common-sense logic snarled at an arbitrary weather phenomenon with a scary-sounding name that could make the whole nonevent sound that much more frightening and threatening. It virtually guarantees a front-page article, and also likely gives the writer a chance at a couple of follow-up stories and interviews.

The news report also had a selection of quotes from eyewitnesses to the ooze rain epidemic sweeping across Europe. The witnesses reported that the rain had begun falling at around 12:30 P.M., seemingly out of nowhere.

"It smelled like a horde of rotting, gutted fish left for days," a man from Finland who witnessed it had said during a live interview.

Neo had to admit that there was no denying it was an interesting story, but the probability was that some unknown chemical plant located in an equally unknown part of Germany had gone all Chernobyl and was spilling toxic yellow-red ooze into the atmosphere.

Knowing Germany's track record for reporting these type of accidents, well, it would likely be months or even years before the guilty chemical plant and its leadership was located. Even then, the Germans would maintain their *"turn the other cheeck"* policy of not taking responsibility for their actions.

Neo took another nonchalant bite of her sandwich and noticed more people were sitting at tables around her who had made their way into the café for lunch. She glanced at the digital clock on the wall behind the counter, which displayed 12:34. She began the process of shutting her laptop down, packing it up, and hopping on her bike for the ride back to the *Times* to turn in her article to the editor well before deadline.

Outside the café's window, she could see the daily bustle of life in Los Angeles continuing as it had for decades. The people changed, the buildings got dirtier from smog and taller, but it all boiled down to people getting on with their normal lives, doing the best they could to survive and strive.

Neo loved that type of city vibe.

"How was everything?" the Greek man behind the counter asked her. "Mouth watering as usual," Neo responded. "Glad to hear it. That's going to be $9.65," he said. She swiped her credit card and autographed her signature, pocketing the receipt in a coin pouch she carried.

"Have a wonderful..." he stopped mid-sentence, his eyes peering over her right shoulder, out to the street behind her.

"What's going on out there?" he asked almost to himself. Neo noticed a confused expression engulf the man's face as she twisted around to see what he was talking about.

Through the window, she could see heat waves bouncing off the sidewalk and the street. Instead of the usual LA hustle and bustle she had noticed only minutes earlier, she saw that many of the pedestrians were now strangely standing still. Most were shading their eyes against the bright Los Angeles sun as they gazed skyward.

"What the hell?" Neo slowly muttered to herself before taking a step closer to the window. From the cloudless sky, a yellow-red substance had begun to fall with the force of a light shower. The drops pattered onto the scorching sidewalk, and began collecting into small gooey puddles.

A thick glob of it splashed against the café window and startled Neo. Her first thought was that it looked similar to exposed brain particle. She watched it slide slowly down the glass as it seemed thick and sticky. She suddenly had an inkling of how appropriate "ooze rain" was after all. In the span of a minute, the light shower increased to a heavy downpour.

The ooze rain pummeled the sidewalks, streets, and buildings beyond the confines of the café. It clung to the glass of the window like thick mud, or more appropriately, like small chunks of someone's brain from a horrific, deadly car accident. Gravity slowly pushed it down the window-pane, leaving a bloody trail of ooze behind. More drops hit the window. Some became larger and smacked the window with enough force that Neo could hear the eerie *thump* of the impact against the glass.

Pedestrians, who had until moments before stood gazing in confused fascination at the freakish spectacle, scattered and ran for any shelter they could find. Some held briefcases or purses over their heads as they sprinted under awnings or into doorways and stores. Within seconds, everyone caught outside looked like victims from a *chop 'em up* horror movie, their thin summer shirts blood stained and any exposed area dripping with ooze, which seemed capable of adhering to anything it came into contact with.

Neo strained her neck closer to the café window to try and get a better view. It was difficult to see clearly because the buildings were too tall, but she could just make out a patch of clear blue sky high above the rooftops.

There were no clouds that she could see, and no sign of any aircraft that could have been dumping this ooze rain in an act of Bioterrorism. So much of it was now falling that large pools of ooze had begun to overflow building gutters that spewed bloody waterfalls onto the streets and sidewalks below like severed arteries.

A sudden *thud* caused Neo to give a yell of surprise and leap back from the window. Something large had hit it and fallen, flapping to the pavement just outside. It was a pigeon, covered in ooze rain. The half-blinded bird had flown straight into the café's storefront window.

The bird, with one wing noticeably broken, flopped around and convulsed in a circle for a few seconds, twitched, and then lay motionless on the sidewalk as Neo stood in shock after witnessing the pigeon's final moments of life.

She jerked her head up from the dead pigeon in time to see more birds dropping from the sky. They spiraled down like careless autumn leaves, bouncing off of car roofs or hitting the sides of buildings, then falling into the road where many were promptly crushed under the wheels of the few vehicles still moving.

Neo wasn't sure, but she thought she saw crows mixed in with the dying pigeons. She then noticed something even larger. Was that a seagull? Whatever it was crashed into the windshield of a parked car across the street, setting off the anti-theft alarm.

Just as suddenly as it had all begun, the ooze rain onslaught began to slow. The harsh patter faded away to nothing, leaving behind solid pools of strange ooze clinging and dripping like sludge from every exposed surface, and four million horrified Los Angeles residents, visitors and the like.

***

Within minutes of the ooze rain halting its attack on Los Angeles, some of the people slowly began to abandon their shelter. Others, in complete contrast, decided to err on the side of caution, choosing to remain exactly where they were rather than risk being caught in another bloody downpour.

Neo could see their wide eyes peering out from inside their vehicles and under awnings, while others had their faces pressed to windows staring up at the sky, their mouths wide open or moving a hundred miles an hour, verbally expressing why, what, and how of what the hell just happened.

Neo's heart rate slowly began to return to normal as she continued to watch, choosing to stay behind the seemingly safety of the café's front door, afraid to venture away from the shelter that it provided. Those of a more curious nature had begun examining the remains of the bloody storm – which, from what she could see of the puddles outside the café, appeared to be slowly evaporating into the early August afternoon heat.

Her natural reporter's investigative instinct finally got the best of her as she cautiously opened the door of the café and stepped out onto the sidewalk to take a closer look.

"Holy shit."

Dead birds lay everywhere, hundreds of them, their bodies littering the streets, sidewalks, buildings, parked cars and other vehicles. Each body of a bird was silhouetted by a halo of the slowly dissipating ooze that covered it. It took another couple of minutes for Neo to realize she was missing a perfect opportunity for an *exclusive* story. She pulled her backpack from her shoulder, snatched her Canon camera from its case, and began shooting a panoramic HD video of the surreal scene.

After she had recorded enough footage, she switched the camera to regular photo mode and began taking close-ups of dead birds, pale, shocked faces of bewildered residents, and, most importantly of all, the now fast disappearing remnants of the ooze rain. A few drops of it still hung from the handlebars of her bicycle. She took photos of it as it slowly dripped into a small puddle around her front tire.

Through the microscopic zoom of her camera, Neo could see that whatever the ooze rain was, it wasn't simply evaporating or being absorbed into the pavement like normal rain. Instead, it seemed as though it was breaking apart into smaller pieces.

As she continued to shoot footage of the puddle, she saw one piece simply disintegrate into hundreds of tiny red particles that flipped and somersaulted like a fish out of water on the street's warm currents of air before spiraling away like a small tumbleweed.

"What do you think that was?" asked a middle-aged woman standing next to her, causing Neo's head to snap sideways and away from her observation. The woman had taken shelter under the awning of a bookstore next to the café. Yellow, reddish streaks stained her thin blouse, and Neo could see droplets of ooze still clinging to the woman's hair.

"Where did it come from? There wasn't a cloud in the sky before it happened as far as I could tell," the woman said.

Neo pondered her question before offering a reply. "I have no clue, lady. None at all."

OOZE

2

NEO STEPPED BACK into the café.

"So what the hell was that stuff?" the owner asked, remaining safely behind his counter.

"Your guess is as good as mine," she answered. The old Greek nodded as if she had confirmed something he had already known.

"This just isn't natural," he said to no one in particular.

Neo had been meticulous about not touching the ooze, carefully stepping around the puddles on the sidewalk and making sure none of it made contact with her skin. However, there was still the issue of it on her bike handlebars and seat. She wasn't about to touch it if she could help it.

"Can I grab a few of these?" she asked the owner, pointing at a container of sanitizing wipes on the side counter.

"Yeah, yeah," the man said. "Help yourself, but leave some for me. My car is parked out back, and who knows what condition it's in right now."

Neo pulled several of the wipes from the plastic dispenser and walked back out to her bike. She methodically, nervously wiped down the handlebars, leather seat, the crossbar and frame, making sure to toss the used sheets into a trash can outside the café. Satisfied with cleaning her bike, she climbed onto the seat, gave the café owner a thumbs-up gesture and a wink, and began pedaling back to the direction of the *Times* offices.

Soon, the daily routine of Los Angeles had begun to shift back to normal, as if the downpour of ooze rain from the afternoon's empty blue sky was an everyday occurrence and not something that should cause LA to stop dead in its tracks. As they say in Hollywood, *the show must go on*. On the streets, the normal grind of vehicles continued as it did every day.

Horns screamed as pedestrians jaywalked and drivers' tempers flared. Neo concluded that things were likely as bad on the freeways of the city as well. Tourists wandered aimlessly along the *Hollywood Walk of Fame*, staring in store windows, taking pictures, and filming video segments, perhaps to later be uploaded on YouTube.

On her way back to the *Times,* Neo spotted residual effects of the ooze rain in puddles on the sidewalk, on stained clothing, dripping off of baby carriages, and even on the occasional face of a horrified passerby. She also noticed that the air was full of barely visible particles of yellow dust, floating carelessly and floating past her like pollen.

While the majority of Los Angeles had seemingly shrugged off the event, Neo sensed this was no normal day. She knew, with sure certainty that clung to her like vice-grip pliers, the world would remember this day, and those that followed it, for as long as there was still a living human race.

***

There are few things more disheartening to a reporter than to walk into a paper's newsroom and find it silent. It's where the stories are made, formulated, and researched. It's where the magic happens. On any normal day, no matter what time a person walked in, the room would be a controlled commotion of journalists running back and forth consulting in corners, or answering ringing phones. The newsroom is the beating heart of any newspaper in the world.

As Neo pushed through the double doors into what should have been a room full of chaos and noise, especially given the incredible meteorological events she had just witnessed, what slapped her in the face instead was the equivalent of a library reading room.

Pausing for a moment, she scanned the room. While the day shift of thirty-plus reporters and editorial staff all seemed present and correct, instead of being at their desks eagerly piecing together that evening's edition, they had all gathered in groups around the five 60-inch TV screens mounted on the walls of the room.

On a normal day, each TV would be tuned to a different major national or international news channel, ready to catch any breaking stories that may have escaped the paper's ever-watchful staff. Right now, every screen showed NBC. The reporting staff, all the way up to the senior editor herself, stood silently watching as others reported on a developing story that, on any other day, they would be relentlessly pursuing.

No one noticed Neo as she entered the newsroom. There was none of the usual banter or greetings from her friends and colleagues. In fact, not one pair of eyes shifted from the TV screens to her as she moved to her cubicle and dropped her backpack on the desk.

There were only a couple of possible reasons for the *Times* to come to a halting stop, especially this close to a deadline. The first was that no one had witnessed the event that had happened less than an hour ago. Neo instantly dismissed that theory because it was obvious everyone must be aware of what had just happened.

She could see from the reddish stains on her co-worker's clothing that some, like her, had been away from the office when the ooze rain fell. The second reason, and Neo found this difficult to fathom, was that a news event even more earth shattering had supplanted the one she thought would be the biggest event to demand a paper's headlines since the 9/11 attacks, and that idea scared the shit out of her.

"Neo? Where have you been? You okay?" The barrage of questions from Cole Parker, one of the *Time's* assistant editors, broke her introspection.

"Yes. I've been out. I'm fine," she told him before taking a deep breath to calm her nerves. "What's going on? Did you see what just happened?" she asked him, her hand fluttering toward the window.

Cole ignored her question.

"Come on over here," he demanded. "You need to take a look at this, right now."

Not waiting for Neo to comply, Cole grabbed her by the elbow and guided her to the group crowded around the nearest TV. On the screen, a female international NBC news correspondent was talking to a young man via a laptop satellite videophone connection. His frightened face filled a box in the top right corner of the screen, giving the appearance he was talking over the news correspondent's shoulder.

A caption under the image of the man read, "Serge LaFleur." Neo estimated that he was no more than twenty-five, maybe thirty, tops. His eyes were bloodshot and revealed a barely restrained panic that belied the calmly delivered answers he was giving to the correspondent's questions.

"Exactly what's going on there? Can you describe what you're seeing?" the news correspondent asked him. When the young man spoke, it was with heavily accented English. Neo guessed he was either French, or maybe French Canadian.

"Everyone is very, very sick," Serge said, his face so close to the lens of the camera, Neo could see the pale, almost translucent quality of his skin. Red veins stood out on his forehead and a spider's web of tiny broken blood vessels seemed to be spreading from his left temple to his cheek, ending just above the man's dark mustache.

Neo could see beads of sweat dripping down his forehead and slowly down his face. When he turned his head for a second and looked away from the camera, she saw more of the ruptured blood vessels on his neck. His eyes were filled with thick lines of red, and deep pockets of blood had collected in the corner of each eye until little of the normal white remained. He was beginning to look like a boxer who'd just taken a brutal twelve-round beating.

"People are dying here," he said frantically. "Many people. They are becoming sick, and then they just die. I see them on the streets, in their cars. There are many, many dead here."

"When you say that there are many deaths, how many? Can you tell us?"

The man paused for a second before replying, "Everyone," he said. *"Everyone* is dead." His voice stuttered slightly as the horror everyone knew he felt momentarily flashed across his face.

"Look, I will show you," he continued. The screen wobbled as he picked up the laptop and carried it a short distance before turning the lens to face out through a second-story set of bay windows. It was nearly dark wherever Serge was broadcasting from, but light from several street lamps cast enough light for those gathered around the TV to be able to make out a tree-lined street with rows of two-story houses on either side.

The houses, nothing but dark square-shaped silhouettes, looked European in design. There were several cars randomly parked in the road. A white truck was resting half on the sidewalk, its rear end straddling the curb of the road, a telltale stream of exhaust fumes floating up from its still-running engine.

"What are those?" a *Times* reporter next to Neo asked, pointing to several dark, almost indistinguishable shapes on the TV screen scattered randomly on the sidewalk and in the road. One of the shapes was slumped against a streetlight.

"Are those bodies? Shit! Those *are* bodies!" The panic in the young reporter's voice made his words rise in pitch as he uttered each expletive.

Neo quickly counted at least twenty unmoving shapes lying in the street. It was impossible to distinguish their gender from this distance, but she could see one that definitely looked small enough to be a child. Next to the child a larger form lay spread-eagled on the pavement, one arm seemingly reaching out to the lifeless body of the child.

This was bad, she realized. This was really bad.

The view on the screen switched from the street back to the face of the young man and a gasp of astonishment mixed with horror escaped from many of those watching. In the few seconds the camera was focused on the unfolding disaster outside, the linear marks in the man's eyes had spread until no white could be seen at all. His eyes looked like two pools of clotted blood.

The network of veins Neo had noticed earlier had doubled in thickness and now extended across his entire face. A delicate web of veins appeared suddenly on his cheeks and a steady stream of thick bloody mucous began flowing from both of his nostrils.

Perhaps it was just her own fear reflected back at her but, despite the obliteration of his eyes, which were now nothing but black pits, Neo thought she could still see the terror he was experiencing captured in them. As the group continued to watch in morbid fascination, Serge's mouth opened and closed once as though he was struggling to speak.

Instead of words, a thick gush of red liquid exploded from his mouth and splattered against the camera lens as he dropped from view, replaced by the image of a background building as the laptop computer toppled from his hands and fell to the ground. A low, gurgling moan filtered through the TV speakers, but it was quickly silenced as the news feed cut back to the NBC correspondent.

The correspondent was visibly shaking, her skin so pale even the layer of makeup she wore couldn't hide it. She pulled herself together and continued her narration. "If...if you're just joining us..." Her words were lost to Neo. A petite brunette *Times* intern standing next to her suddenly began to sob and grabbed for her hand.

"Oh, no! Oh, no!" the young woman gasped repeatedly. Her voice was tinged with a growing tone of panic, and Neo felt the woman's grasp on her hand tighten as tears began to stream down her face.

"Is that going to happen to me?" she said, her voice barely audible as she clutched at her own blood-stained blouse with her free hand. "Am I going to die?"

Neo squeezed the young woman's hand back as firmly as she could. "No, of course not," she said, although she could hear the lack of conviction in her own voice. "We're going to be just fine," Neo reassured her, mustering as much faith to her voice as she was able and reinforcing her weak words with a forced smile.

Cole pulled Neo aside. "Do you believe this shit? Jesus Christ!"

"What about the other news outlets? What are they saying?" Neo asked.

"The same. First the ooze rain comes and then people die. There's been no news from anywhere east of Germany for hours. It looks like the entire population of Europe is fucking dead."

***

"So just what exactly are we supposed to do?" asked Brian Mitchell, one of the crime-beat reporters. Mitchell was in his early seventies, his hair was always slicked back, and he would never be found without his tan raincoat that he wore during the winter and slung over his arm in the summer.

He'd always carry a rolled-up copy of the previous day's *Times* in his free hand. "It adds to the aura," he would tell anyone who asked why he chose to dress that way. Most every other reporter thought he was a little nutty, but Neo thought it was quite charming.

The entire staff of the *Times* crammed into the lower-floor meeting room. Senior editorial management had decided to call a meeting and pulled everyone in soon after Neo arrived back at the office. A feeling of dread permeated the small meeting room, not helped by the overbearing smell of sweat as too many people crowded into too tiny of a space. Senior staff members were already seated around the ten-person conference table when Neo joined the meeting. The rest of the paper's employees were either standing or leaning against the walls.

"It's really up to you guys how we handle this thing news wise," Cole, said. "On any other day, I'd say we stay at our posts. I mean, shit, everyone remembers 9/11; we didn't leave for three days. But this? This is a whole other boat of lobsters."

"I've spoken with both the senior editor and the publisher," Cole continued, "and, while they would obviously like to see today's paper go to print on time, they're watching the TV, too. They told me to tell you it was our choice whether we stay or we go."

Cole looked around the room at the grim faces staring back at him.

"I'm pretty sure I know what the result will be already, but let's see a show of hands for those who want to call it a day and get out of here."

Everyone except Brian raised their hands. He continued to lean against the wall, his arms folded in front of him. He'd left his trusty rain coat at his desk.

"Brian?" The assistant editor's voice was tinged with concern for the eccentric crime reporter.

"I'm staying," Brian replied stubbornly. "I've been with this paper since I stepped foot out of college and I'll be damned if I'm leaving now."

"Jesus, Brian, were you watching the TV? You saw what's happening in Europe. What do you think this town's going to be like if that happens here?" Jayla, one of the legion of proofreaders, said.

"You have to go home, Brian. Who knows how long this is going to last? It could be days before everything gets back to normal."

"The *Times* has been my home for nearly fifty years," Brian shot back. "Besides, there's no one for me to go *home* to. At least if I'm here I can do some good. Don't worry about me. I'll be fine. When all of this blows over, I'll be the first to say, 'I told you so.'" He added a halfhearted smile to his last statement that convinced everyone he wasn't going to budge about staying put.

"All right, people. It's decided. The *Times* is officially closed until whatever this thing is blows over," Cole suddenly announced. "I'll see you all then. Keep your cell phones close. We'll call you when we need you. In the meantime, don't you all have homes to go to and families waiting? Get out of here...now."

The staff began quickly filing out of the meeting. What little conversation there was continued in hushed, subdued voices. Neo stopped at her cubicle and waited, pretending to check through her mail while the rest of the staff grabbed their belongings and headed toward the exit. Finally, when only Cole and Brian were left, she walked over to them. Brian's back was to Neo as he talked with Cole. She pulled on the elbow of Brian's tweed jacket to get his attention.

"Neo, my dear," he said, turning to look at her. "What a day, huh? What a day."

"Yeah, it really sucks, Brian. Listen, why don't you come home and stay with me? I've got an extra room. There's no need for you to stay here alone."

Brian smiled at her, his gray eyes twinkling, "While I appreciate the offer, I'm going to man my post. Besides, I won't be alone. Mr. Parker here has decided to keep me company, haven't you?"

Cole just nodded, and while his mouth smiled, his eyes were unconvinced. "Yeah, someone's got to make sure this old fart doesn't run off with the laptops."

"Are you sure? The both of you are more than welcome to stay with me," Neo offered.

"While the offer is tempting," Brian said, "we're staying. You'll find us right here when you come back. Don't worry, we'll be fine."

Cole smiled and shrugged. Both men looked at her reassuringly. She knew they wouldn't budge.

"Well, take care, you two," she said over her shoulder as she turned and walked back to collect her belongings from her desk. "You know where I am if you change your mind. Just give me a call and let me know you're on your way if you do. Okay?"

She smiled as she caught Brian's whispered words to Cole, "Oh, if only I were forty years younger, I just might take her up on that offer and get all up in that. Life is just so damn unfair sometimes."

***

Neo pushed through the *Times's* revolving doors and stepped out onto the street. The day seemed just like any other, the streets filled with people and vehicles intent on getting wherever it was they needed to be. There was no visible hint of panic or even an undercurrent of unease as she stood for a moment watching.

It seemed the news of the deaths in Europe had not yet reached the majority of LA's occupants. Everything looked and sounded normal. Down the street, near the intersection, she heard the screech of brakes followed by a burst of profanity. While the world was falling apart around them, the people of Los Angeles continued with their day, either oblivious or uncaring of what was happening across the ocean in Europe.

Occasionally, someone would pass her with a look of worry fixed to their faces, cell phones pushed firmly against their ears as they spoke in low concerned tones to those on the other end of the line, maneuvering their way through the crowd and on to some unknown destination. Neo thought she was probably witnessing the slow circulation of the news as it gradually filtered down to the city's residents and tourists.

At some point the spread of information would reach a tipping point among the city's population, a critical mass that Neo knew would turn her town inside out and upside down. As news of the deaths across the Atlantic became common knowledge, people would panic, and then Los Angeles would become a very dangerous place to be caught out in the open.

It was imperative she got home as quickly as possible. She needed to prepare for whatever was heading her way. She had seen enough horror movies in her time to know that whatever came next was not going to be pretty.

Neo moved out into the crowd, cutting diagonally against the flow of pedestrians so she could reach her bike. She released the lock and slid the chain from between the bike's wheels, tossed it in her backpack, checked that there were no taxis using the bike lane as a shortcut, and, when she saw it was clear, began pedaling toward home and the familiar comforts of her apartment building.

***

Twenty minutes after leaving the *Times* offices, Neo pedaled up to the outside of her apartment block. She locked her bike to the security stand out front and headed inside. The lobby was busier than it should have been at this time of day, a sure sign, she thought, that news of the deaths sweeping across Europe had finally begun to filter onto the city's local radar.

A group of five people waited nervously in front of the elevator. They looked frightened, more so than she had seen anyone since leaving the newsroom. She wondered how much information had actually trickled down in the time it had taken her to get home.

She recognized a couple of the tenants waiting in front of the elevator and almost said hello, but she noticed stains from the ooze rain on their clothes and thought the better of it, choosing instead to simply nod, smile, and keep what was hopefully a safe distance between them and her.

She had managed to keep herself free of any contact with the ooze rain so far. She didn't know if that would matter in the long run, but it was probably better not to take any chances and to stay as far away as possible from people who had been caught in the downpour.

She had no way to tell how the agent, or virus, or whatever this ooze rain turned out to be, had killed those people in Europe, or how it was spread. For all she knew, it could be airborne and simply breathing the same air or touching a doorknob used by an infected person could mean the difference between life and death. In fact, it was a good idea to avoid enclosed spaces like the cabin of the elevator, and avoid any contact with possibly contaminated people, period.

"Jesus!" she said aloud, surprised at how little time it had taken her survival instincts to label everyone a potential threat to her life. She felt guilty for thinking that way, but how else was she supposed to think? Less than two hours ago, she had witnessed live on TV a man die a horrible death. If that same outcome was in store for the people of Los Angeles soon, she was sure as hell going to do whatever it took to guarantee it didn't happen to her.

With that thought on her mind, Neo opened the door to the emergency stairwell and began climbing the stairs up to her apartment on the seventh floor instead of taking the elevator.

OOZE

3

NEO KNEW HOW LUCKY she was to have snagged her apartment at Bunker Hill Towers on S. Figueroa Street, perfectly situated a couple of blocks from Grand Park in downtown Los Angeles.

It was a stone's throw from some of the most amazing restaurants in LA. It was also handy for major public transportation hubs, if she needed it. It was rare, but sometimes interviews for articles took her outside of her comfortable biking range.

The rent for her apartment was well outside what Neo would normally be able afford on a journalist's salary, but she was approved for an unbelievable price after she had written a flattering article about the owner of the management company who owned the apartment complex. Her article had helped him fill vacant apartments and he was pleased with her for helping him. To show his appreciation he had given her a sweet discount. Those are sometimes the perks of the job. Neo certainly wasn't complaining.

Her apartment was a one-bedroom, one-bath on the seventh of nineteen floors. She knew a couple of the other tenants on her floor. Most were single professionals, but there was a married couple in one of the apartments and a single mom with an eight-month-old little boy named Milo, a few apartments down from hers. While the majority of her neighbors were friendly, she knew them on nodding terms only. Everyone kept to themselves for the most part, which was fine by her.

The apartment building had its own gym in the basement area and a covered community pool on the roof. Not that she ever had the time to use either, of course, but it was nice to know they were there if she ever decided to take advantage of them. Besides, her daily bicycle commute was more exercise than the majority of people got in a month.

Neo grabbed a bottle of water from the fridge and walked into the living room. The far wall was framed by a large bay window that looked out over the nearby rooftops and beyond. She was secretly in love with whoever had designed her apartment because they were smart enough to include a seat beneath the window where she could sit and watch the world pass by.

She called the little area her *chill zone*. It was just a wooden bench with a thick layer of padding and a pastel-blue cover, but it was one of her favorite places to sit and unwind from the many and varied stresses that she encountered at her job on a daily basis.

She kicked off her shoes and sat down on the bench. Pulling her legs up to her chin, she took a long drink of her water and stared out over Los Angeles. While most of her view was blocked by a row of equally tall buildings positioned between her apartments, she could still see the tree-lined shore of West LA in the distance.

Until today, Neo had always thought of the sprawling metropolis of Los Angeles as a microcosm of the United States, a multicultural melting pot with very different parts that, despite their differences, worked together for the common good of all. It was laid back, it was fast, and it was unapologetic. It had been unstoppable in its continual forward movement. That all changed today. Not since the dark days of 9/11 had she seen so much fear on people's faces.

Neo stared down at the street. The buildings were mainly older office blocks, but sprinkled here and there was the occasional small store. Within walking distance, a hungry professional could find a coffee shop and a convenience store. Just across the street and around the corner from where she lived, a small candy store kept a stock of chocolaty goodies to satisfy any sweet tooth.

As Neo's her eyes roamed the buildings, she saw a flurry of motion in the street below. A group of about twenty people had gathered in front of a newspaper stand. At this distance, there was no way she could hear what the group was saying, but their body language was unmistakable – they were pissed.

Fingers were being pointed, fists clenched, and people were being pushed and getting up in each other's faces. Most of the anger seemed to be directed at a single man, who stood directly behind the stand, his hands raised to the side of his head, palms out, as though he was telling the angry crowd to stand down. The crowd, which seemed one wrong word away from being reclassified to mob status, apparently wasn't having any of it.

Neo thought she saw a fist connect with the man's jaw and then he disappeared in a mass of flailing arms and bodies as the crowd pushed their way forward, surging through a narrow doorway of a small clothing store behind the newspaper stand. Seconds later, she watched as people began running from the store, their hands full of the shop's clothing.

She watched a man trip and fall, the shirts he carried spilling from his hands as he sprawled into the road, narrowly avoiding a speeding SUV that barely managed to swerve around him. The vehicle didn't even try to brake. By the time the man raised himself to his feet and dusted himself off, others had already grabbed everything he had stolen. He stood dazed in the middle of the road, then took off running up the street, quickly disappearing from her view.

Neo had seen plenty of disturbing incidents during her time at the *Times,* but there was something uniquely upsetting about the scene she had just watched play out seven stories beneath her window. She felt helpless and alone. It was like watching someone she dearly loved succumb to madness, and there was nothing that she could do to help.

The sound of knocking at her apartment door took her away from her thoughts. She wasn't expecting company and figured it was Cole and Brian. They must have changed their minds and decided to take her up on her offer to stay with her.

"Coming," she called out as she walked to the front door.

The management company for the building was big on security, so every apartment front door was equipped with a peephole. When Neo placed her eye to the viewer it wasn't her colleagues from the paper; instead, she saw a police officer standing outside her door.

***

Neo unlatched the security chain and opened the front door. The cop was a good six-two, with sandy brown hair cut so short most of it was concealed beneath his cap. A name tag over the left breast pocket of his uniform jacket read *Carlson.*

"Nick? Thank God you're here," she said, giving him a kiss on the cheek. "Have you heard what's been going on? Do you know anything?"

He didn't answer. He instead pushed past her into the apartment entrance and then turned to face her.

"Shut the door," he said abruptly, his usually calm voice laced with an edge of panic she had never heard before.

"C'mon, Nick. Not even a hello?" Neo replied, allowing anger to creep into her voice, more to cover her own uneasiness than because she was truly annoyed at him.

"I'm sorry, babe," he said. He leaned in to kiss her firmly on the lips. When he finally released her, she took a single step back and stared up into the face of her boyfriend.

"I thought you were on duty today."

"I'm supposed to be," he answered as he walked toward the kitchen, "but Neo, it's crazy out there. I couldn't even get within a mile of the precinct. Everyone's leaving LA and heading out of the city. The roads are jammed, people are rioting, looting, and going berserk."

He stepped around the counter to the kitchen, opened the refrigerator, took out a bottle of water, quickly twisted the cap off, and downed a huge gulp.

"I tried calling the lieutenant," he continued, "but the lines are all busy. I thought I'd check on you and hole up here for a couple of hours until the roads clear, and then I'd head back in."

They took a few minutes to talk about what they knew. Nick had seen the same newscast as his girlfriend and had no more information than she had.

"How bad do you think it will get?" she asked eventually, trying to keep her voice from displaying the panic she could feel in the pit of her stomach.

"Honestly, Neo, I don't know. But shit, did you see the ooze rain? I had just left the precinct when it came. There wasn't a cloud in the sky. You're the reporter...how do you explain that?"

She couldn't, of course. She'd seen the same phenomenon and had no idea how the ooze rain had fallen from a clear sky. "I can't," she finally said, and moved around the counter to join him. "All I know is that I'm glad you're here." She reached out and took hold of the lapels of his jacket, pulled him to her, and kissed him again.

As she released him, Neo felt something wet on her hands. She glanced down at them and gasped as her heart sunk to her feet when she felt red ooze on the tips of her fingers, and the dapple of red covering her blouse.

"Oh, hell no!" she said in disbelief. She bent down and grabbed a bottle of Clorox bleach from the cupboard under the sink.

"Shit! Shit ! Shit!" she whispered in panic. She jammed the plug into the drain, emptied the entire liter container of bleach into the sink, tossed the empty bottle onto the counter, and plunged her hands into the bleach. She counted the seconds off in her head, one-thousand-one... one-thousand two...one-thousand three...

Only after she was sure her hands had been submerged for at least thirty seconds did she pull them out, just long enough to grab a scouring pad from the counter and begin scrubbing furiously at the red stains still on her hands.

After all the precautions she took, after managing to avoid contact with the ooze rain all day and everyone who might have come into contact with it, she'd been faked out by something as simple as wanting to kiss her boyfriend. Neo began to sob quietly to herself as the full weight of the day finally broke through a crevice of her consciousness, delivering an emotional sledgehammer blow against her chest.

"Jesus, babe. Are you okay?" Nick was at her side, a hand resting gently on her shoulder. She spun around and knocked his hand away. "Why didn't you tell me you had that shit all over you?" she yelled. Nick flinched and took a step back. While the couple had experienced arguments since being together, he'd never seen her as upset or as angry as she was now.

"You should have told me. Why didn't you tell me?"

"I...I'm sorry," he stuttered. "I didn't even think..."

Neo looked up at Nick's horrified face, his concern for her was so obvious and his reaction to her fear was so like him. It was a big reason why she fell in love with him. They had met just over two years earlier at the scene of a multiple-car pileup. The accident claimed the lives of a young family of three, along with two other drivers. The man that had caused the crash, drunk well beyond legal limits, of course, had walked away with only a few scratches.

"How romantic is that?" she would usually tell people who asked how two seemingly polar opposites had gotten together. The truth was, Nick was the only cop she had met in all her years on the job who was still moved by the arbitrary nature of destruction, loss of innocent life, and the pain he witnessed on a daily basis. Unlike other cops, Officer Nick Carlson still knew how to *feel*. He retained a human heart, and he wasn't afraid to show it. In the often-dark world both he and Neo inhabited, well, that was a trait she found exceedingly attractive.

Nick had no problem with her occasional use of profanity, as her mother would call her ability to swear like that of a rapper. Dating was hard enough in LA, finding someone to put up with her large vocabulary of swear words was even more exceedingly difficult.

Neo felt the anger subside. She stepped in close to Nick and threw her arms around his waist, sinking her head onto his chest, aware that she was probably opening herself up to more contamination with this simple act of intimate contact, but not caring anymore. She knew she had deluded herself into a false sense of security from the moment she set foot outside the safety of the café after the ooze rain had fallen.

The world was literally falling to pieces, and she was trying to act as though it was all okay, as though she was somehow beyond it. Her mind screamed at the thought of all the suffering this could bring. She buried her face deeper into Nick's chest, smelling the musk of his sweat through the layers of his uniform, fighting the urge to cry.

Dark waves of fear created an avalanche through Neo's body. Weakened by the panic that held her firmly within its grasp, she felt her legs turn into mush. She just couldn't hold back anymore as tears welled up and began to trickle down her cheeks. Nick let her lean against him, resting his cheek against the top of her head until her sobbing gradually began to slow.

***

Neo could not think of any other time in her life when she had been this afraid. She simply wanted to curl up into a ball until everything was back to the way it should be. She had never been one to simply give in to fear, and she certainly wasn't going to start now, she told herself, despite what had just happened, but she was now in survival mode and found it difficult to resist.

Nick had finally managed to connect with the police department and had spent the last several minutes stalking back and forth through the apartment while he spoke in a hushed voice to whoever was on the other end of the line. When he was finished, he slipped his phone back into his pocket and joined his girlfriend in the living room.

"They're canceling everyone's leave," Nick said, sitting next to her on the couch. "They aren't telling us much other than the city's going into a full lock down."

"Is that just here or the whole state?" she asked, blowing her nose into a tissue that Nick handed her from a supply he kept in his jacket pocket. He considered her question for a second. She knew him well enough to know that when he was pondering whether he should divulge a piece of sensitive and private information.

"Christ, Nick. It's not like I'm going to run off to the *Times* and publish your every word. You can't hold out on me with this. Not now. Not today," she said.

"It's not that I don't want to tell you or that I don't trust you," he said. "It's just that I don't want to scare you any more than you already are. Besides, the intelligence we have isn't much more use to you than what you're seeing on TV. The lieutenant told me the word is that they're preparing for massive casualties.

The Center for Disease Control and Prevention has absolutely no idea what to do. They can't even figure out what that ooze shit is, let alone what it's going to do to us, so there's no chance of a vaccine. They don't know how it's communicated or why it does what it does."

"So what are we supposed to do while they all sit on their asses? Just wait and hope for the best?" she asked.

Neo jumped up and began searching for the TV remote. She found it sitting on the kitchen counter and pressed the power button. The TV was tuned to a movie channel from the night before. It was playing a fifties science fiction flick, so she quickly tapped in the number for the local news station. Not surprising, the anchors were talking about the ooze rain: "... there seems to be confirmation that the news out of most of Europe is as devastating as we have thought. The president issued a statement just a short time ago.

"While there is no reason to expect the same problems here in the United States, I recommend that citizens practice an abundance of caution and avoid anyone who has come into contact with the ooze rain until the Centers for Disease Control and Prevention has had time to analyze samples and can determine exactly what we're dealing with," the anchor said.

Another anchor went on to say, "The president went on to say that he thought it best if everyone return to your homes and remain inside for the next twelve hours. Reports are also reaching us that National Guard units across the country have been mobilized to help deal with any disturbances, and to ensure the security of major population centers. Going back to our main story, all contact with Europe and German leadership appears to have ceased approximately eight hours after the first reports of the ooze rain. However, news agencies across the U.S. have received numerous videos and messages apparently depicting mass casualties from countries including the United Kingdom and Italy.

"Similar incidents of the ooze rain phenomenon have been reported across the continental U.S., Canada, and

South America. Again, if you're just joining us, the president of the United States has announced that—"

Nick turned the TV off. "I'm not reporting for duty," he said. "I think it's better if we just ride it out right here."

"They'll fire you, Nick," Neo said, surprised that he would be willing to risk losing his job.

Nick thought about what she said before answering. "I don't care," he said finally. "Besides, I don't know if there's even going to *be* a job to go back to."

***

"Babe, how much food do you have?"

Nick's question left Neo dumbfounded for a moment because she hadn't even given her supply of food any thought. Her job wasn't your standard nine-to-five, so most days she would eat lunch at her desk or at the nearest café, as she had today. When she got home, she would usually grab something light like a salad or a sandwich. She didn't exactly keep a well-stocked pantry.

She checked the shelves, taking an inventory of what food she did have: a six-pack of instant soup, a six-pack of ginseng tea, a couple of cans of fruit, a can of peas, and a can of mixed vegetables. There was a half a loaf of eight-grain bread in the bread basket on the counter.

The fridge held the remains of a quart of low-fat milk, an almost-full bottle of orange juice, a half a pack of glazed baked ham, enough fresh vegetables to make a couple of decent salads, some leftover pasta from two nights earlier, and four cans of Miller Lite beer. It wasn't what anyone would call a stockpile, but it would be enough to last them a couple of days until the calamity settled down.

Nick apparently didn't agree with her assessment because when he saw how much food was left, Neo had to stop
him from leaving her apartment and heading out to the
store to pick up more supplies.

"You can't," she said. "It's not worth the risk. We have
to minimize our exposure, and you running off to the store
is only going to heighten our chances of getting sick. We
can survive for a couple of days on what we have – we'll
just have to be careful." She paused for a second then added
with a coy smile, "We'll just have to find other ways to take
our mind off the lack of food."

Nick seemed on the verge of leaving anyway. Neo
reached out and took his hand in hers. She could see the
frustration written across his face. He was a man used to
acting in situations, to being in control, a problem-solver
who was now faced with an insolvable problem.

"It's okay," she said, squeezing his hand. She saw the
look of anxiety on his face, but that quickly transformed
into a smile. He leaned in and kissed her gently on the lips,
then placed both hands on her shoulders and held her at
arm's length, looking deep into her eyes. "I love you, Neo
Kao," he said.

"I love you too," she said, and then pulled him close and
kissed him again.

***

There was little real news on any of the TV channels.
Most of what was being broadcast was just speculation
or reruns of video and audio collected from webcams and
phone messages recorded at the time the effects of the
ooze rain hit Europe. Then there was media sensational-
ism, and lots of it.

Depending on whom a reporter was interviewing, the ooze rain was either a big hoax to try to frighten the American people into paying more taxes for healthcare, or a *Houston, we have a problem* episode from NASA. No one actually knew what was happening as it was all speculation, but mainly it was depressing and incredibly frightening.

After an hour of staring at the same talking heads on TV, Neo switched channels and searched for anything that would take their minds off what was going on outside the apartment. She settled for a rerun of the classic, *Gone with the Wind.*

After they both took a shower, Neo and Nick sat next to each other on the sofa and allowed themselves to watch the movie in silence and be soothed into a sense of normalcy, her head resting against his shoulder, his hand resting in her lap. Her eyelids became heavy and, rather than fight it, she allowed the gentleness of the moment to sweep over her. Within minutes, her eyes closed and she fell asleep.

***

Neo awoke dazed, unsure of where she was. It took her a moment to realize she was stretched out on her sofa. Nick had placed a thin shawl over her, but he was no longer sitting next to her. For a brief moment, she thought he had decided to take a risky trip out to the store for supplies but, as she sat up, she heard his voice from behind her.

"Hey there, sleepyhead. How are you feeling?" She sat up to face him. He was standing in the kitchen working on a cup of coffee.

"Want a cup?"

"No, thanks."

Neo then stretched and stood up, placing the shawl on the arm of the sofa. She glanced at the stove's digital clock and realized she had been asleep for nearly two hours. At some point during her preemptive nap, Nick had switched the TV back to NBC. He had lowered the volume to just above a whisper.

The news anchor spoke in an urgent, rapid tone, but he didn't have anything new to add and was just repeating the same news she had already heard. Neo was reaching for the remote to switch the TV off, still tired of feeling afraid, when she noticed something odd.

The anchor was bleeding from her nose. It started with just a few drops splashing onto the pile of loose paper she held in front of her, then quickly turned into a consistent drip. It took her a couple of seconds before she realized she was bleeding.

She dabbed at her nose with her right hand, a look of surprise and embarrassment crossing her face as it came back bloody. She began to apologize for the unscripted interruption but stopped mid-sentence as the blood suddenly streamed from both of her nostrils. Her hand dabbed her nose to try and stop the bleeding, but the blood was flowing so quickly it ran straight over the back of her hand and between her fingers.

"Ladies and gentlemen, I...I'm terribly sorry about this..."

She began to cough, pulling in huge gulps of air, then to choke, her face was turning as white as the blood-splattered sheet of paper she still clutched in her free hand. Neo could see the fear in the anchor's eyes as she, and probably several million people across the country, realized what they were witnessing. With a sudden spasm, her hands flew back, exposing her throat and the thick bright-red engorged veins pulsing beneath her skin.

A violent muscle spasm snapped her upper body forward, and her face and chest smashed into the desk, sending a spray of blood flying across the room. A droplet of blood hit the camera lens and slid slowly down, leaving red smear behind. The woman convulsed again, her body flying back into the upright position. Her eyes stared directly into the camera as a slow wet gurgling sound escaped from her throat.

Her microphone picked up screams of terror from the studio staff but they were barely audible above the sound of the TV anchor as she slowly drowned in her own blood, her body gripped by violent convulsions as though she was in the midst of a massive seizure.

A thick red stream of blood exploded from her, spilling across the news desk. She continued to shake violently for a few seconds and then abruptly stopped. Her jaw fell open and she exhaled a long sigh as her head slumped forward until her chin came to rest against the lapel of her blood-stained blouse. The screams the microphone picked up as the anchorwoman died in front of everyone's eyes had been replaced by the sounds of faint gurgles and cries.

Neo realized she was trembling. "Oh my God," she cried, through hands clasped tightly to her mouth. "Damn! Nick? Are you watching this? Dear God...it's here."

She turned to look back at Nick. Her boyfriend was still standing in the kitchen, his face pale with shock. His blood-shot eyes locked on hers as a stream of red gore exploded from his mouth, flooded onto his shirt, and began to form a red pool on the carpet.

OOZE

4

NICK WAS DEAD on the kitchen floor.

His body lay slumped against the wall next to the refrigerator, a large pool of blood slowly thickening next to him and on his ooze-covered uniform.

Neo wasn't sure how long she had stared at Nick's lifeless body. It must have been awhile, because the screams and cries of the dying she heard filtering through her walls from surrounding apartments had finally, hauntingly, stopped.

The loud suffering of her fellow residents registered in her mind only in passing. Neo's attention was solely on Nick as he collapsed and began to convulse. His left leg twitched, causing his shoe to bang against the refrigerator.

Each time his shoe struck the refrigerator door the cuff of his jeans inched up a bit, revealing the nearly translucent skin of his leg. Bulging veins pushed against the skin; engorged with blood. It seemed as though the veins were ready to burst from his body.

The walls of her kitchen, now blood-splattered, told the story of the violence of Nick's final seconds on earth. There was so much blood. Streaks of blood covered the counter, the cabinets, and the floor. But there were no wounds on Nick's body, just his open mouth and a slow stream of blood dripping from it. His eyes, wide-open and black with death, stared off into nothingness. Dark droplets trickled down his cheeks like tears as clots of blood collected in the corner of each eye.

Knowing she had touched the ooze on Nick's jacket, Neo waited for her turn to die.

Death was soon coming for her, too. She was sure of it, and waited. It would be just a matter of seconds before she joined Nick and the millions of victims across the world who had already become victims of this violent, insidious, ooze plague.

The inevitability of her death came as serenity for Neo, a calmness within her mind as everything complicated in her life became unimportant. Her only responsibility now was to wait. She hoped it would happen quick, and wouldn't hurt much.

She stared at the clock on the stove as the minutes ticked away; first ten, then fifteen, then thirty. She would catch glimpses of the clock and see that time was still passing and she was still alive. *Hurry it up already, will you.* She thought.

She lifted her hand to her nose periodically to check for the telltale nosebleed that would commence her coming death. The first time her hand came back bloody, she began to sob quietly and wiped the blood away with the sleeve of her blouse as she waited for the pain to close in on her.

When she checked her nose again, there was nothing but dried blood on her skin. She began to realize it wasn't her blood – it was Nick's, which likely splashed across her face during his final seconds of life as she watched in horror her boyfriend convulse and slump lifeless to the floor. She knew there was nothing she could have done to help him.

Everything was dreamlike and distant. Neo wasn't even sure who she was anymore, or whether this was reality or just some horrible nightmare. Other than the systematic hum of her ceiling fan and her rapid breathing, there was nothing but silence now. The constant background noise that she had become so accustomed to became noticeably apparent by its surreal absence.

The constant stomping feet of the couple and their crying baby above her apartment, the distant metallic grinding and whoosh of the elevator as it moved from floor to floor, the screech of tires on the street outside her apartment, had all ceased. As LA's residents and visitors died, its essence had died with them. All that remained was crushing, unmitigated silence.

Neo realized this was the first time she could remember ever hearing herself breathe, or the noise of the icebreaker in the refrigerator as it pushed frozen cubes into the dispenser. Even on those rare sleepless nights when she found herself awake at 3:00 A.M., the city was still alive. She still had been able to hear the traffic outside the apartment, or the sound of a TV from other apartments drifting to her ears.

Now there was *nothing*.

Los Angeles had been silenced forever.

OOZE

5

AN HOUR HAD PASSED since Nick died.

Neo's feeling of calm began to disappear as she slowly began to surface from her mind's self-imposed Houdini state.

She was alive...but not well.

She tried to stand, her legs cramped, and she staggered back down on the floor, the pain driving up the calves of her legs. She crawled over to the coffee table and picked up her cell phone. She finger tapped an icon on the screen of her phone and dialed 911. "Come on," she whispered. "Please. Come on. Somebody answer."

The phone rang, then several more times, and yet again. No one answered.

She hung up in frustration and immediately dialed the number to the front desk at the *Times*. It rang four times before a woman's recorded voice answered and said, "If you know your party's extension, please dial it now."

No one answered the phone at the front desk. She realistically had not expected anyone to be working the reception area. Everyone except for Brian and Cole had left, so the system had defaulted to after-hours mode. She dialed Brian's extension number.

It rang three times before she heard his voice. "Hello. You have reached the desk of Brian Mitchell. If you would like to leave me a message..." Neo hit the pound key on her phone and the system returned her to the main menu. "If you know your party's exten..." The recording cut off when she tapped in the two-digit number for Cole's extension.

It went to voicemail message, also.

She methodically dialed every extension number she could think of. Each time the voice of her friends and colleagues greeted her and asked her to leave them a message, that they would get back to her as soon as they could. She sensed that was never going to happen again. She stared at the phone in her hand, hoping it would ring, and for someone, anyone to call her back.

There was one more call she needed to make. Slowly, she dialed the number to her Dad and Mom's house.

Neo's father and mother had retired twelve years earlier. After selling the farm, they had packed up and moved to Phoenix, Arizona. "Gotta get it while the getting's good, "her Dad told her in his best John Wayne drawl during one of her annual trips back home. "We're craving some sun and warm weather," he had gone on to say. "After sixty years of living in Montana, I think we both deserve it, don't you, sweetheart?"

Neo had agreed. It was the best move they could make, but she still felt some sadness at the loss of the home she had grown up in, and, despite her childhood desire to leave Big Timber as soon as she was legally old enough to, the idea of never going back there had been painful.

Listening to the phone ring with no answer from her parents, she remembered how happy they were the last time she had seen them. They each flaunted a deep tan from too many days in the Phoenix sun. Neo teased them about having acted like a couple of teenagers, holding hands, cuddling up on the sofa together as they talked with their one and only child.

When Neo heard the answering machine click on, she let out a deep sigh, fighting back an avalanche of tears at the sound of her Dad's voice: "Hey, there! You have reached Phil and Tina. We can't come to the phone right now, but if you'd like to leave a message, we'll get back to you as quick as we can."

At the beep, Neo spoke softly into the phone. "Dad? Mom? If you get this message, I'm okay. I'm alive. Nick is dead. I think everyone else here is probably dead, too. I hope you're okay. *Please* call me soon. I love you."

As she tapped the off button to end the call, she was left with the disheartening feeling that she would likely never talk to or see her parents again.

***

Neo stepped into the hallway outside her apartment. "Hello?" she called out, her voice echoing along the empty hallway. "Can anybody hear me?"

There was no answer, just the gentle hum of the air-conditioning. From somewhere on the floors above her, she thought she heard the sound of music playing, but she couldn't be for sure. She had already tried flipping through the local TV channels but found nothing except desks and pre-programmed shows.

"Hello?" she yelled again, louder this time, but still no one answered her.

Neo stepped back inside her apartment and walked toward the kitchen. She grabbed her keys and put them safely in the front pocket of her jeans. She then turned and retraced her steps back to the front door, opened it, and stepped outside again. The click of the lock engaging when the door closed behind her made her heart pound as panic was about to set in. Thankfully, she ignored her fear and began to walk down the hallway toward the elevator.

There were 225 apartments in her building. She made her way to her nearest neighbor's door, knocked loudly, and rang the apartment doorbell.

"Hello?" she shouted. "Is there anyone in there? Can you hear me?" Placing her ear against the cold wood of the door, Neo listened for some kind of an answer, something that would tell her that she was not the only one alive. There was no reply from any of the other apartments, not even the bark of the Yorkshire Terrier or Dachshund she knew two of the neighbors on her floor kept as pets. She walked over to the next apartment and repeated the process. After the fifth door remained closed, she stopped knocking.

She decided to venture further down the hallway as she walked carefully, searching for any signs of human existence. Set back in a nook off the main corridor, the waiting area for the elevator was hidden from view until she rounded the final corner.

Neo then discovered the second shock of a lifetime.

The twisted body of a dead woman lay half in and half out of the elevator doorway. Every few seconds the automatic doors would try to close and then spring back open as they thumped loudly against the woman's lifeless body.

The woman lay face down, her head and upper torso resting on the glossy cement floor of the hallway. A large amount of dried blood spread out around her head while a portion of her body remained inside the elevator. Two plastic bags of spilled groceries lay at her feet. The items, mostly canned Chunky soup of different varieties, and two plastic liter bottles of Pepsi, had erupted from the bag when the woman fell to her death, and now lay scattered over the floor of the elevator.

The petite dead woman was dressed in an expensive-looking black business suit. The jacket and white shirt beneath it had ridden up around her midsection, exposing the small of her back and the myriad of tiny engorged veins creating an ugly latticework across her pale skin.

One of the dead woman's hands lay outstretched in front of her, her fingers cupped as though she had died while trying to drag herself out of the elevator. Her other arm was pinned beneath her body. An expression of sheer horror was engraved on her face.

Neo had actually seen her share of dead bodies in her time in Los Angeles. It came with the job description of being a metro-reporter. Most had been the result of automobile accidents, suicides, or a murder. She thought of herself as a hardened newspaper veteran at the sight of a dead body, but how much more could she take?

She surely wasn't going to leave the poor woman just lying there. It was too disturbing and wouldn't be the right thing to do. Neo stood over the body for a few moments before deciding what she had to do. She placed the heel of her right sneaker against the dead woman's shoulder and pushed.

The body moved a few inches, revealing a red smear of blood, but then it stopped as the friction of the elevator's rubber-lined floor made it impossible to push her any further. There was only one way this was going to get done. Neo would have to pull the body into the elevator by its legs.

She strategically stepped over the body, carefully avoiding the pool of blood and avoiding the doors as they once again tried to close and then sprung back open. Neo half expected the woman to suddenly reach out and grab her foot like in a horror movie. She paused and had a mental image of herself being dragged kicking and screaming into the elevator, the doors sliding silently shut, and her screams slowly fading down the empty hallway as the elevator moved to the next floor to pick up other living riders to feast on her flesh.

Snap out of it, girl, and get a grip.

Neo grabbed the woman's legs by her stylish black pumps. Whoever this woman was, she had taste *and* money. Neo tugged on the woman, and her body made a nauseating slurping sound as she dragged the body feet-first the remaining distance inside the elevator.

She had expected the woman to have a level of rigor mortis by now and was surprised at how much flexibility there was in the dead body. She lifted the cuff of the woman's trouser and pushed it back, exposing the woman's ankles and a few inches of the calf of her leg.

Although the woman's skin was pale, it didn't have the gray ash she had seen in other dead bodies. There also didn't appear to be any noticeable discoloration either. Neo was no doctor, but she was pretty sure that was part of the normal course of human decomposition. Perhaps she was wrong in this case.

Neo was so engrossed in her thoughts that she hadn't noticed the dead body was now completely clear of the elevator doors, which promptly began to close again. Neo gasped in fear of being caught alone inside the elevator with the dead woman and taken to the next floor beyond her will, thrust her hand between the metal door and frame in time to keep herself from being trapped in a moving metal coffin. When the doors opened again, she jumped out from the elevator cabin to the safety of the hallway. The elevator door then closed free of obstruction as Neo stared at the dead woman's curled fetal-like body in the corner inside the elevator.

She watched the red glowing LED numbers on the floor indicator rise through the eighth, then the ninth floor, finally stopping at the tenth floor.

***

The door to apartment thirty-seven was open. Neo's heart began to beat faster as she approached it. Perhaps there was someone alive in there. Not wanting to walk into the apartment unannounced, she leaned toward the crack of the door and yelled out, "Hey! Is there anyone home?" As she leaned her head in, her shoulder nudged the door open farther, and the sudden squeak of its non-oiled hinges startled her, setting her heart racing once again. She composed herself and pushed the door wider as she stepped into the apartment.

A light in the short hallway was on, and Neo could see the curtains pulled closed in the living room at the opposite end, burying it in darkness. The apartment was stylishly furnished. Freshly cut carnations housed in an expensive-looking vase rested on a table near the sofa.

Beneath the sweet scent of the carnations was an unmistakable funk. She recognized the odor of vomit mixed with the metallic, heavy tang of spilled blood. It wasn't too strong at this end of the apartment, but the open door allowed the air-conditioned hallway to pull the stench toward her.

Neo walked farther into the apartment's hallway. She didn't bother announcing herself again because she was convinced she would find more dead bodies. Where the hallway opened into the living room area, she noticed a small shape of a body sprawled on the floor. It was a child, no more than two or three, a young boy. His dead, black eyes stared at the ceiling and a small fist gripped at the blood-soaked Disneyland T-shirt he wore.

In the dead boy's other hand was a small brown teddy bear. A dark pool of blood, leading from his nose and mouth, had dried around his head. His mouth hung loosely open and forever locked in a state of shock and terror, the same expression as the dead woman in the elevator.

Neo flashed her hand to her mouth and tried to stifle a cry of horror. She tried to avoid looking at the little boy as she stepped around him, her eyes focused on two other seemingly dead bodies. The bodies of two adults lay near the small boy.

The man, apparently the father, was still sitting upright on the living room sofa, his eyes and mouth wide open and his arms hung loosely at his side. His head drooped toward his left shoulder and a stream of dried blood and vomit poured from his mouth down the front of his navy blue pin-striped business suit, forming a black pool of liquid death in his lap. It appeared as though he was watching the news on a flat screen TV fixed to the far wall of the apartment before he died.

A woman, Neo assumed it was the boy's mother, lay crumpled on the floor in front of the man. When she collapsed, she had apparently fallen through a glass coffee table, smashing it into a thousand pieces. Shards of broken glass were everywhere, covering the floor in front of the sofa. A larger piece of glass protruded from between the woman's left arm. The larger piece must have severed one of her arteries as the pond of blood surrounding the woman was much larger than the ones she had seen from the other victims of the ooze rain.

Curled up on a mat in the corner of the room, Neo saw the family dog. It too was dead. This sickness, this ooze plague, didn't seem to discriminate between species, and she knew she may not have seen the worst of it.

Viruses weren't supposed to transfer between species she had thought. This one, however, seemed more than capable of killing anything it came into contact with. She remembered the dead birds she had witnessed falling from the sky when the ooze rain first fell. If the ooze rain was able to kill across species, then where would it stop?

Would it mean that every creature on earth was affected, or only those that had come into contact with it? She wondered why she herself was still breathing. Why didn't the ooze rain kill her like it did the others? Neo suddenly felt overwhelmed with so many questions, and very few answers anywhere to be found.

She closed her eyes tightly to keep herself from contemplating beyond the surface. For all she knew, this was simply a localized viral outbreak and help was already on its way. If that were true, then she wouldn't have to worry about what kind of a threat the ooze rain was.

She could leave it to the experts to figure out, not her. She was just a journalist. Neo knew her line of reasoning was shaky at best, but it was all she had, and at least for now, she was going to hang onto it at all costs. She began stepping backward toward the front door, being careful to avoid looking at the bodies of the dead family.

In the hallway outside, the cool of the air-conditioning flowed over Neo. She wanted to move her search to the other floors of the apartment building. She walked up to the elevator, and without thinking, nearly pressed the call button before she realized that would only summon the dead woman back to her floor.

She remembered the news footage she had seen of the devastation in Europe. It made her realize that her very own survival was a complete oddity. Everyone else was most likely dead, both here in her apartment building and throughout Los Angeles, most likely even across the country, and perhaps, as difficult as it was to allow herself to consider, the world.

If there happened to be survivors in her building, she certainly would have heard *something* from someone by now. One of them would have been walking or running, searching for others as she was. One thing she was sure of, she wasn't going to put herself through the pain and horror of finding more dead bodies.

Neo stood in front of the door leading into the emergency stairwell. She pulled open the door and yelled into the open entrance, "Is there *anybody* here? Can anyone hear me?" She waited a few seconds for an answer she knew wouldn't come, only the ghostly sound of her own voice echoing back to her and the metallic clang of the door as she let it close behind her. Despondent, she walked slowly back to her apartment.

On the long walk back to her apartment, Neo noticed four bright red pull-station activators for the complex's fire alarm system. Each floor had them strategically placed in case of an emergency. She had passed two of them before a great idea smacked her upside the head. She now had a perfect solution and stopped at the one nearest her apartment.

Embellished with the word *"FIRE"* in large yellow letters on each case, the alarm could be triggered by simply pulling down on a small plastic handle. If there was anyone left alive in the building, or even nearby for that matter, she figured this would be the best way to let them know there were other survivors, or at least cause them to come out of their apartment.

Still, Neo was reluctant to activate the alarm system. It wasn't like she was yelling fire in a crowded mall. This *was* an emergency, and it served as the only way of ensuring that she would get the full, undivided attention of any survivors left in the building.

She gripped the handle with her fingers, took a deep breath, and pulled it down. A white strobe light set high up on the wall began flashing instantly. It was accompanied by an ear-splitting alarm that was so loud it forced her to throw her hands to her ears in pain and panic.

"Dammit!" she exclaimed while at the same time allowing herself a slight smile of triumph. If *this* didn't get someone's attention she didn't know what would. With her hands still firmly covering her ears, Neo sprinted back to entrance of the emergency stairwell.

She opened the door and positioned herself partly in the doorway where she could see anyone who came down the stairs while still having a clear view of elevator floor indicator. If the indicator lights changed, it would mean someone was using the elevators to head to the main floor.

The piercing electronic cry of the alarm quickly induced a numbing headache. In spite of that, she waited nearly twenty minutes in the stairwell, hoping someone might show up. However, the illuminated floor number above the closed elevator door showed no activity, and not a single person met her on the stairs. Still, she gave it another ten minutes before allowing herself to let go of the hope of others being alive in her building.

Fighting back a steadily growing surge of gloom and desperation, Neo let the door close behind her as she walked back to the refuge of her own apartment.

OOZE

6

NEO UNLOCKED her apartment and stepped inside. She walked slowly into the kitchen to get a bottle of water and froze when she saw Nick's body lying there.

Strangely, she had completely forgotten about him the second she had left the apartment. She knew it was because of the trauma of the entire event, but it was way too much for any person to be able to comprehend.

She didn't know how to cope with it all because for now, there was no one to help her. The sound of the fire alarm was somewhat silenced by the walls of her apartment, but it was still loud enough to be a constant annoyance, especially as her headache was growing into a mind-numbing, full-blown migraine.

Neo realized that she hadn't thought through the whole activate-the-fire-alarm plan quite as well as she thought she did. She was obviously blinded by the false hope of finding someone else who had survived the ooze rain.

It was all just too much for her overworked emotions to deal with. She was tempted to simply let go of reality and allow herself to regress and forget about the disaster she found herself in. She theorized, however, that if she were to allow herself the luxury of skipping out on reality, the chances were she would never come back. She could feel herself standing on the very brink of total insanity, and who could blame her.

"No," she said through a clenched jaw. "That's not going to happen. I'm not going out like that."

She quickly dismissed any thought of giving up. Neo was a survivor. She had *always* been a survivor, and she sure as hell wasn't going to change now simply because it seemed as if the world was imploding right before her eyes.

She shook the cobwebs out of her head and walked with a purpose toward the bedroom, doing her best to push the sound of the alarm from her mind and focus on the task at hand. She opened the linen cabinet, pulled out a spare pair of bed sheets, and tossed the top sheet back in the cabinet, choosing the elastic-edged fitted sheet instead. Fortunately, it was a king size, Anything smaller would not have been effective for what she had in mind.

Neo walked with the sheet back to Nick's body and deliberated about how she was going to do what she needed to do. He was sitting upright, which would help, but he weighed nearly two-hundred pounds, and she knew she wasn't strong enough to completely lift him – dead weight and all, or carry him to another room in her apartment if things didn't go as planned.

She let most of the sheet to drop to the floor while she kept the top hem stretched between both of her hands. She looped the edge over Nick's head and forced it down between his shoulders and the refrigerator that his body leaned against. She had to press her right knee against his chest so that he wouldn't keel over too soon.

She pulled the elastic edge of the sheet first over Nick's right shoulder, and then the left, being sure to push it down as far as she could until both the right and left edges met. She tucked the side edges of the sheet underneath his elbows and pulled the remainder of the sheet down over his feet. With the sheet securely in place, Neo shifted to the side of Nick's body, gripped the edges of the sheet together as tightly as she could, then pushed against her dead boyfriend's shoulder.

Nick's body slowly slid sideways down the refrigerator until he lay flat on the floor.

Neo had to give the edge of the sheet a couple of tugs to pull the right side free so it met the opposite side. She grabbed his legs at the ankles, straightened them out, then moved back to his shoulders, still holding the edge of the sheet together, and pushed. Nick's body roller over and rested face down on the kitchen floor, completely wrapped within the fitted sheet, leaving him mummified.

She had already figured out exactly where she was going to put his body. She decided to take Nick's body to the apartment where she had found the dead family. It was farther in distance, but it also seemed more of a respectful thing to do for Nick, instead of her initial thought of stuffing him into the elevator with the dead woman she found earlier.

She found a roll of twine in the kitchen utility drawer and cut several three-foot lengths of it. She slid the first piece under the sheet near Nick's head and slid it down until it was parallel with his wrists. She then tied the two loose ends together, securing his arms to his sides within the shroud. She repeated the process again to secure his arms at his shoulders, and to lock his ankles firmly together.

When she was finished, Neo crumpled up a handful of the fabric near his feet until she had enough to give her a secure hand a good grip. She tied that off with a shorter piece of the twine. She then gave the sheet a couple of strong tugs to ensure Nick's body was secure within the sheet. Satisfied, she took hold of the hand grip with both hands and began to pull his dead body toward the front door.

Neo was able to effortlessly slide Nick along the smooth tiled kitchen floor, but when she got to the carpet, it made moving his body more strenuous.

By the time she pulled Nick through the front door and out into the seventh floor hallway, she was sweating and breathing heavily. She dropped Nick's feet to the floor and took a moment to catch her breath. The alarm, so much louder in the hallway, slammed against the front of her skull like a mallet.

When she reached the halfway mark near the elevator, her head felt as though it would create an explosion of its own ooze at any moment. The muscles in her arms and back burned. Her fingers ached in every joint where she had gripped the sheet tightly to keep it from slipping out of her hands.

She was tempted to leave Nick's body right there in the middle of the hallway for the night, but the idea of facing him first thing in the morning was incomprehensible. Neo interlocked the fingers of both of her hands and flexed them until her knuckle joints popped. She then reached down and continued to haul Nick's body toward the waiting door of apartment seven nineteen.

***

Neo bumped the door of the apartment open with her ass. She pulled Nick's body down as far into the apartment entry as she could before her hands cramped in pain, causing her to let go. Nick's sheet-covered feet slammed down on carpeted floor with a thud, and Neo slumped right over him, huffing and puffing as her back rested against the wall, allowing air to fill her lungs again.

Her curly dark brown hair had matted to her forehead and she pushed it back out of her stinging, sweat-filled eyes. Her head was thumping to every beat of her heart, her vision was blurred, and her ears felt like they were engulfed in flames. She had never felt so much pain and exhaustion in her life, not even from working on her parent's farm in Big Timber.

It took all of her willpower not to close her eyes and fall asleep right then and there. Instead, she boldly raised herself to her feet, knowing there was still much work to be done, while ignoring the pain in her back and knees as she hobbled out of the apartment.

At the front door, she paused for a moment and gazed at the mummified form of Nick's body. "Bye, babe. I love you," she whispered in mourning, and pulled the door shut until she heard the click of the lock engage.

Neo had taken two steps toward her apartment when the continued raging of the fire alarm stopped all of a sudden. There was a moment or two pause and then she heard four short, sharp beeps as the system had either shut itself down or reset.

"Thank you, Jesus," Neo said as she wobbled back to her apartment.

***

Her headache gradually subsided, but only after she downed a couple of painkillers with a can of beer from the fridge. Unfortunately, no amount of alcohol and pills was ever going to ease her numbing grief over the death of Nick.

She sat facing the window of her apartment, sipping the remainder of the Miller Lite while she stared aimlessly out at her little slice of Los Angeles, watching the sunset slowly crawl over the buildings. Neo had never experienced such a profound silence before, both outside the apartment and within her heart, mind, and soul. She found it unbearable in trying to comprehend it.

The streets of Los Angeles were free of people and animals, yet littered with abandoned vehicles. The sky, usually buzzing with aircraft from LAX and birds, was vacant and clear. It was quite beautiful, actually. A light brown haze of smog still swirled high above the rooftops, the only reminder of the millions of lives that had passed through the streets and alleys below, only hours before.

A dusk gradually edged toward night as Neo watched the streetlights begin to flicker silently on, casting long shadows that stretched and grew before being absorbed in the descending darkness.

The stillness soon became intolerable, and Neo abandoned her perch at the window for the sofa instead. She turned on the TV, mostly for the comfort gained from filling the room with any sound other than her own breathing. The image of the dead news anchorman stared back at her on the TV screen, his eyes, black and lifeless. She returned his stare for several minutes, turned the TV off, and limped to the bedroom.

As she passed through the kitchen, Neo took a glimpse of the bloodstained pool where Nick died and the splatter on the counter and the walls. She was too tired to clean it up right now as it would have to wait until morning. She dejectedly plodded into her bedroom and collapsed on top of the comforter.

Within ten minutes, she was asleep. Thankfully, she didn't have any nightmares.

OOZE

7

The Next Day...

NEO WOKE AN HOUR before dawn and watched the birth of a new day from the same window she had watched its death, this time with a cup of black coffee in her hand instead of a beer. Her body still felt the pain of abuse that she had put it through the previous evening, but it felt better this morning.

Her body clock had opened her eyes right on schedule for her to get up and get ready for work. As those few groggy seconds between sleep and full wakefulness wore off, it erased the cobwebs piercing through her mind. Yet, the previous day's events cleared into terrifyingly sharp focus.

Reality had snatched Neo out of her bed, and she had run excitedly to the living room window like a small child on Christmas Day who had expected to rip the wrapping paper off and open up glorious holiday gifts.

Just in case, she thought to herself. *Just in case what had happened really was just a bad dream.*

As she passed by the kitchen, she glanced down at where, in her bad dream, Nick's body was, and where the blood stain should be. It wasn't there. It was *gone*. Not a trace left. She raced to her perch at the window, threw back the drapes, pressed herself against the cool glass, and stared out at the *still* empty streets and sky of Los Angeles.

Neo stood at the window, watching what should have been, even at this early an hour, a bustling city filled with office workers, joggers, bike riders, dog walkers, tourists, street vendors, and everything that made Los Angeles the only place in the world she would ever want to live. She glanced back over her shoulder at the kitchen and the location where the blood stain should be. The blood was gone for sure. Nothing remained.

Nick's police-issued bomber jacket lay on the sofa where she had left it yesterday, and his cap sat on the kitchen table. Nick *had* been there. He *had* died here. Yet, that didn't explain why his blood had disappeared from the floor. Neo examined the floor and the walls in the kitchen where she thought the blood stain had been. There was no sign of it. It was as though it had never existed.

She didn't remember cleaning it up, but, perhaps in her stress-induced state of mind, she had left her bed in the middle of the night and removed it. After what had happened yesterday, she surmised that anything was possible. She didn't think it was likely that she would have done that, and the blood certainly didn't clean itself up.

Outside the window, the dawn sky was a fiery red above LA's rooftops. With each passing minute the morning sunlight brushed back the shadows that had owned the streets, but there was little consolation for Neo. The streets were still empty.

She began to feel the last of the cobwebs clear from her foggy brain. She decided that she needed a plan, some kind of strategy for figuring out how to get in touch with authorities and law enforcement to inform them that she was alive. There had to be other survivors out there. It was just a matter of finding them, that or leaving enough clues to help them find her. She didn't care which came first, as long as one of them came in a hurry.

Neo walked back to the kitchen, found her backpack nearby, and pulled a notebook and pen from it. For the next hour she diligently worked on compiling a comprehensive to-do list. Telephone numbers, email addresses, physical addresses, social media sites, anything she could think of that would help her reach out and locate other survivors.

She had to adhere to a strict timetable of calling the numbers on the notepad every couple of hours. She could use the time in between to check news websites and the TV for any updated information, that is, if anyone was out there and alive to deliver it.

There was no way for her to tell how long it would take a rescue squad to barging in over the horizon, so she would need to find supplies to get her through the next couple of days. She mulled over the idea of visiting some of the apartments on other floors, but she thought the chances where high that it would only end in the same result as she had on her own floor yesterday, more dead bodies.

If there was anyone alive in the building, the fire alarm would have certainly brought all but a deaf person running. Even then, a deaf person who could see would have high-tailed it out of there.

Neo wished she had been more sensible yesterday to grab what supplies she could from the dead family's apartment. That was not an option now as she had clearly heard the door lock behind her when she closed it after dropping off Nick's body, and she was still too tired and sore to even attempt to break the door down.

Thus, she was going to have to take a trip in the city and grab whatever provisions and survival gear she could. It would also serve as the perfect time to get some *fresh* air as the putrid smell of dead bodies was beginning to grow stronger. She needed to make a few calls before she ventured outdoors.

Neo had compiled a list of numbers to dial and listed them in order of priority of the probability of someone answering. She picked up her cell phone and dialed the first number on her list, listening as the phone at the other end of the line rang four times before picking up.

"You have reached the White House. If you know your party's extens..." Neo hung up and dialed the next number. No one answered at the Pentagon, either. She tried the numbers for the FBI, the CIA, the Smithsonian, the Center for Disease Control and Prevention, and every police precinct and hospital within a fifty-mile radius. When she exhausted California's state political party headquarters, she moved on to the numbers in Los Angeles City.

The only voices she heard belonged to dead people.

At about three in the afternoon, her bladder was full from drinking coffee and several bottles of water, causing her to stop dialing numbers and use the bathroom. She realized she could also use a nice hot bath, but that could wait until later in the day.

She was getting hungry too, so she decided to take a break and grab a bite to eat. She warmed up a can of clam chowder on the stove and added a few saltine crackers to it. She ate her lunch quickly and quietly, and then returned to her phone calls, choosing key numbers in Dallas this time.

By four-thirty, both Neo and her cell phone battery were close to empty. She hung up from her last call, tapped the off icon button on her screen, and almost threw it at the wall in frustration. Instead, she walked into the kitchen and attached it to the charger she kept permanently plugged into a wall socket.

It would take about an hour for it to fully charge, so now was a good time venture away the comforts of her apartment to go grab the supplies she needed. When she got back, she could start working on browsing the social networking sites for any signs of life around the world.

Got to stay positive and keep a smile on your face, sweetheart, the memory of her father said inside her head as she grabbed her keys from the kitchen counter and headed out the door.

OOZE

8

NEO STEPPED ONTO the concrete terrace outside her apartment and gazed up at the clear sky.

After a day of being holed up in her apartment with only artificial light, the sudden and welcome exposure of natural sunlight was much appreciated. For the first few minutes, as she acclimated herself to being outside, Neo could almost believe that nothing had really changed. As the sounds of a ghost city echoed, she began to sense just how truly profound a change had swept over Los Angeles.

Besides the gentle rustle of a nearby flag on a pole, there was no sound at all. There were no people, no music, no dogs barking, no birds chirping, no couples talking, no babies crying, just a metal graveyard of abandoned vehicles of all makes and models scattered along the street. The only sounds that she could hear were the rhythmic beating of her heart, and the quietness that seemed to quadruple the weight of the air around her, which had now become maddeningly annoying.

When Neo was a child, she had gone on a school field-trip to a petting zoo. The school bus was jam packed with kids. All the way to the zoo and all the way back was filled with the nonstop, innocent chattering of the children. The bus was abuzz with conversation and life.

When the field-trip had ended, the school bus driver dropped the kids off directly outside of their homes. Neo lived the farthest away and hers was the last stop. By the time the bus driver pulled up outside her parent's home, the bus was empty, except for herself and the driver, who wasn't ever overly talkative on the best of days, and even less so after spending hours with a bunch of hyper kids. The blast of voices of forty or so kids that had filled the bus quickly dissipated, and young Neo had felt the first disquieting sense of stillness, and how life can suddenly change.

Now, as she stood outside in the sunshine of what should have been a beautiful Los Angeles day, Neo had the same sense of stillness she felt when she was the last kid on the bus, but multiplied a billion times. All sound had left the city, and in the void it left behind, there was nothing but pure, peaceful, perfectly and agonizingly *horrifying* silence.

Los Angeles smelled different, too. It smelled...clean. That quintessential aroma of LA – a mixture of carbon monoxide, burgers, hot dogs, dry cleaners, coffee shops, bakers, mixed with the sweat of four million people, had also vanished.

***

Ocassionally, after a heavy rain, Los Angeles almost smelled that way, like crisp fresh laundry. It would linger for a few minutes, but even then, there was always an underlying taste to the air that never really disappeared...until now. This morning the city smelled sterilized and the air tasted sugary, free of all the pollutants, dirt, and everything else that made it so special to Neo, that gave it its unique character and essence. Now it was all gone.

Her apartment served as a buffer against the desolate circumstances that now covered a silenced Los Angeles like a humongous umbrella, shielding her from the power of the true gravity of the emptiness that surrounded her.

Neopolitina Kao – possibly the *only* human being alive for miles around.

She felt the weight of the reality passing deep within her soul. Neo also realized that she was, quite likely, the sole witness to something so bizarre that no other human had ever experienced before – the death of an entire civilization, perhaps the entire human race.

"*Fuck!*" she shouted out loud, startling herself with how loud her voice sounded as it bounced off the empty concrete terrace. "*Fuck!*" she said again, glancing around the empty street. "What the *hell* am I supposed to do now?"

What happened to everyone? There had been plenty of warnings in the after-hours the ooze rain had fallen for even the most technologically unconnected of the Los Angeles residents to learn what was going on in the rest of the world, and decide whether to stay or go home.

Shortly after the ooze rain landed, the news would have quickly trickled down to every level of the city. People would have been faced with the choice to stay or leave. Most of them it seemed, had decided to go home to their families, where they obviously felt safe and protected.

There may be other survivors who happened to be stranded around LA, or perhaps even some that had taken refuge in their offices or businesses. There could be thousands of people just like her who had survived and had decided to wait it out for a couple of days to see how things panned out, in the hopes of being found alive and rescued. Reality set in Neo's mind once again. She figured that if there had been other survivors, they surely would have tried to make others aware that they were alive, as she had done.

It just didn't feel right to her. As strange as it sounded, she had no sense of anyone else being alive due to the distinct lack of life and spirit within Los Angeles. The very air, so crisp and clean now, felt deprived of energy. It seemed as if the very beating source of life in LA had suddenly vanished. Life as she knew it on earth had come to an astonishing halt.

Directly across the street from Neo's apartment building was a row of offices and small stores. As she scanned the buildings for any sign of life, her eye caught an undistinguished shape curled up in the recessed entryway to the candy store.

It was difficult to make out exactly what it was from where she was standing, so she took a few extra steps closer. Stopping short of the curb, she instinctively glanced both ways before stepping into the street.

She stopped in the middle of the street, and stared at the shape in the doorway. It was a body. She could now see a pair of scuffed brown boots sticking out from beneath two blankets.

"Hello?" she yelled out. "Are you okay? Do you need help?"

There was no reply and no movement from the blanket-covered body. Neo took a few more steps toward the doorway, stopping when she came about ten feet away. She could make out the shape of a person's body beneath the tattered, dirt-stained blankets covering everything from the head down, except for the old boots. It appeared as though whoever was under it had curled up in the doorway and pulled the blanket up over his body to either sleep the night before, or take cover when the ooze rain hit the city.

Frightened, Neo took a deep breath, and then walked the few remaining steps until she was standing next to the huddled body. She reached down and slowly lifted one frayed edge of the blanket.

The man beneath it was dead. He looked to be in his late fifties. A thick beard streaked with gray covered his chin, along with a bit of stubble across his cheeks. His skin was tanned dark brown from too many years exposed to the bright California sun and a knot of tiny blue veins extended across his nose and cheeks.

A half-empty, cheap bottle of red wine was held tightly in his right hand and clutched against his chest as if the bottle was the most precious possession in the world to him. It took Neo a minute to realize that there was no blood on the man. The only substance noticeable to her was a fine yellow-red dust that covered his head and face.

The dust also coated the man's top blanket. When Neo pulled the blanket farther down his body, the tiny dust particles floated gently up into the air, then slowed and began to fall back toward the dead man, settling back on his exposed skin like a dog or cat finding its way back home after wandering off.

As she watched, she observed more of the yellow-red dust float down and settle on the pale skin of the man, as if his corpse had some type of a freakish magnetic charge that attracted the dust to him.

It wasn't just the yellow-red dust that she had caused a stir on the blanket that Neo could see migrating toward the dead body. More of the dust was floating in from outside the candy store's entrance. The afternoon sunlight streaming in at just the right angle caused her to notice it slowing moving toward him. She remembered how the ooze rain had dissipated yesterday, and how it had broken apart and floated away rather than evaporated.

An impulse overcame Neo. She blew a strong breath toward the particles floating around the entrance of the candy store. Her breath pushed the tiny dust particles back to the street. Strangely, instead of being swept away from her, the dust slowly began to float back toward the dead man's body as if he was its mother, or in this case, its father.

The dust particles weren't simply floating, either. Neo saw them actually migrate diagonally, as if powered by some inner entity and drawn toward the dead man's skin. Neo look down at her T-shirt, her jeans, and her sneakers. She then shook her head vigorously in an attempt to shake any of the dust out of her hair. There was nothing. It had not tried to adhere to her body any way, form, or fashion.

She continued to observe, in a matter of seconds, the entire exposed portion of the dead man's face became buried under a layer of yellow-red dust to the point she could no longer make out any of his features. Neo was fascinated by this phenomenon. It was if the man was wearing a colorful mask.

Once the yellow-red dust touched the man's skin, the particles jostled and wiggled with each other for position, rearranging themselves so they filled in any exposed areas of his skin. She resisted the urge to touch the dust, being fearful of the consequences.

She then came to ponder the probability that by some strange twist of fate, or good fortune of her DNA, why she was a survivor of the ooze rain. However, she didn't feel the need to push her luck. It was bad enough she was likely inhaling the dust with every breath she took.

Neo realized there could be any number of logical explanations for what she had just witnessed. Perhaps the dust was attracted to the man's skin by static electricity. The blanket was made of wool, so when she pulled it back it could have generated enough static to cause the dust to be attracted to his skin. Something about that logic didn't sit right with her. She surmised that if that scenario were indeed true, why didn't the dust just fall upon the dead man's blanket instead of his skin?

She wasn't yet convinced that what she had just seen was real. Neo carefully pulled back the rest of the blanket from his body. Dust particles instantly still wafted in the air near the candy store entrance. The dust circulated and began to make its way to the exposed skin of his body.

The dust was clearly making a beeline straight to his hands. There was no mistaking it. She watched a dust particle that had, until moments earlier, been heading out toward the street perform a circular U-turn before slowly sinking to the corpse and settle into place on the dead man's right hand.

The particle had been about three feet away from Neo, too far to be affected by static. It had unquestionably changed its direction and headed slowly downward before joining the other particles that moved smoothly back and forth on the dead skin and rearranged themselves into a uniform, symetric layer.

More particles fell on the man's hand, and Neo decided to test her experiment a little further. Careful not to create any disturbance to the air, she pulled the blanket back up to the man's chin, while keeping her eyes glued on the descending particles of dust. As soon as the blanket covered his hands, the dust that had been heading toward them slowed and turned lazily in the still air to begin moving back out in the direction of the street.

The thought lodged in the center of her brain like a splinter and throbbed almost as painfully. First the ooze rain, now this weird dust. She had the feeling something far, larger, and more complex than a simple virus was responsible for this strange new world she founder herself in.

She wondered if the two incidents she just laid eyes on were related and if so, how? She knew an expert scientist wasn't going to magically show up and offer her an answer. If someone *did* have some knowledge of all of this, Neo wondered if the answers had died along with them. While she might be the last living human being on the planet, she had an uneasy sense that she was no longer *alone*.

***

As hard as she tried, Neo couldn't shake the idea that something intangible was becoming aware of her. Perhaps it was paranoia, but she felt as if a million hidden eyes had focused suddenly on her, watching her, studying her every move.

Although she knew it was likely an impossibility, the feeling of anxiety that it created proved just as impossible to not consider it. She had no plausible explanation that could explicitly explain the events taking place around her.

The dust swarmed and whirled around the dead man like knats. Neo, though saddened for him, knew there was nothing more she could do and left him. The crazy thing was – there weren't any knats to be found, or any flies for that matter. Why? She had not seen any bugs flying around since the ooze rain. The thought flashed across her mind for a moment before she dismissed it.

All she could do now was to continue on with her plan. She needed to pull herself together and get back on schedule.

Two buildings down from the candy store was the corner convenience store where she had witnessed the near riot in reaction to the ooze rain the day before. The street ghost-like. There was no sign anything had happened except for a few splattered liters of brands of cola outside the store. The door to the store was unlocked. She pushed it open and stepped inside.

Ding-Dong!

When she pulled the door open to the convenience store, she let out a shriek of surprise as the electronic door chime activated.

Neo had spent most of her life feeling good about being prepared for anything. She was a confident young woman in her own capabilities, and focused on staying positive and moving forward just like everyone else she knew. Yet here she was – completely alone and unprepared, and at a complete and pure loss as to what she should do next.

It was ironic that the sole surviving human being, as far as she could tell, would be a journalist. The largest news story in history and there was no one left alive to tell it to. It was simply too much for her to envision.

Her legs felt like butter as they were ready to buckle under duress of her circumstances. Neo shook her head in despair, followed by more fear, and tears. She tried to suppress the emotion but she couldn't. She covered her face with her hands and began to cry aloud at the thought of everyone she had loved and lost.

Everything dear to her was gone. It was swept away from her in an instant. It left her no time whatsoever to say goodbye to loved ones – especially her parents and Nick. Gone also was music, television, the theater, her friends and co-workers, her career – everything that made life worth living had been stolen from her, and those who died, in just one day, leaving her alone and deeply saddened.

Her sobbing turned into a wail of despair as she knew that none of those things would ever be coming back. Humanity was gone, finished, snuffed out in a single day like a Los Angeles gang-related drive-by shooting.

Her shoulders heaved and shuddered as the collapsed to the cold floor of the store, knocking over a stand of magazines and sending them slithering over the tiles. She picked a magazine up and tossed it at the door, with a yell in pure frustration. She felt her body shrink to the floor again, curling herself into a fetal position as the pain just kept coming.

A few minutes later, emotionally washed out, her body exhausted, Neo fell into a deep sleep, hoping she would never wake up.

***

Neo's eyes blinked open. The stiffness in her neck from lying up against a wall on the chilly floor of the candy store meant she was still alive. She felt a bit better, under the circumstances. Purging herself of her emotional burden had released her from its weight and allowed her mind, heart, and her soul to gather the will and strength to unload the pain and fear.

She extended her right arm against the wall and pulled herself to her feet, stretched the stiffness out in her tired legs, and stretched her aching arms as she glanced around the candy store's interior. She had no idea how long she had been asleep.

It must have been at least a couple of hours because the inside of the candy store was darker than when she first walked in. She guessed it must be close to sunset as she stared out through the storefront window. The street lights were beginning to flash on, one by one.

Outside the store, lit up by the glow of the nearest light, she could see a throng of yellow-red dust. The glow of the light turned the dust an apocalyptic black, but what confused Neo was how *much* of it she could see as it floated past the light. A countless number of specs of the dust moved along the street, silently flowing in a unusual rhythmic wave.

What was making it float like that? The wind hadn't even caused the leaves on the nearby trees to dance. The dust seemed to merge into a single giant creature roaming the vacated streets of Los Angeles, searching for a cause only it could know and understand.

The cloud of dust gyrated like the large dragon puppets Neo had once seen at Grauman's Chinese Theatre on Hollywood Boulevard. The enormous dust cloud moved up and down in a contortion style wave past the window. It was a captivating sight. What she was witnessing caused a major shiver to shoot up and down the spine of her back, her arms, shoulders, and her head. It was if she had been momentarily possessed by what was happening.

She walked to the window and stared out at the twisting dust particles. It was only a day earlier that she had stood in the café and watched as the ooze rain had fallen. The world had dramatically changed since then. In her mind, it all seemed a lifetime ago. When the ooze rain fell, her old world, the one where Neo was just another young woman trying to make it through the day unharmed, had died as well.

She resisted the strong urge to speak her thoughts out loud. The temptation to talk to herself was overwhelming, and who could blame her. It was less than forty-eight hours since she had heard another human voice. She never imagined the profound effect it would have on her, until now.

A sense of journalist responsibility came over Neo. She needed to document what had been happening. She even went as far as feeling confident enough to figure this whole thing out. If she didn't at least try, then who would?

"Damn, right," she shouted, allowing a glimmer of a smile to cross her face as she turned her attention away from the odd dust storm raging on the other side of the window, and back to finding supplies.

The candy store had been looted of almost everything. Two rows of metal shelves had once held an assortment of delectable sweets, candies and cookies was now barren. Another of the empty shelves had tumbled over and now leaned against a wall. Neo carefully picked her way through a maze of shattered candy boxes, nuts galore, a variety of colorful, spilled jelly beans and chocolates, all mashed to the floor by the prior stampeding feet of looters.

Behind the cash register was a sign promoting a display shelf that housed discounted gift trays and baskets. It was also empty now. She walked around the counter and through a small swinging door.

Searching for anything in edible condition, she pulled the empty gift tray and basket shelf away from the wall, stepping back to let it fall against the counter. Behind the shelf was a hidden compartment of the store. Neo figured the owner must have used it as an overstock storage area.

It was unlocked, but more importantly, untouched as far as she could tell.

She leaned down and lifted the door hook latch and found several unopened boxes of 1940s retro candy. Her eyes popped open wide. The proverbial *little kid in a candy store*, quite literally, came rushing back to her from yesteryear. Her jaw had dropped at the delicious sight of such retro goodies like Sugar Babies, Heath Bars, Bazooka Bubble Gum, Charms, black licorice, Dots, Bubblegum Cigars, Jolly Ranchers, and more.

She quickly closed the small door back and latched the hook as she looked anxiously over her should as if more looters had come back and discovered her newly found stash of sweets. She walked back from around the counter and to a small room at the back of the store that served as the main stockroom. The battered wooden door was wide open, hanging from a mangled hinge, the imprint of a large boot near the broken lock.

Neo leaned her head into the dark storeroom. She patted the wall until she found a light switch. A single bulb with no shade hung from the ceiling, but it was bright enough for her to see that there was little left to pilfer. The room had been professionally picked over and it was as much of a shambles as the front of the store; the floor was covered in torn cardboard packaging, smashed gift baskets and ripped apart candy boxes.

A plastic jug of water caught Neo's eye. It was the kind of container of water one would find in an office break room, where employees would gather around the water cooler and gossip about their bosses and co-workers.

The jug had rolled against the near wall of the stock-room. She made a mental note to come back for it later if her current apartment water supply ran out as she rolled it to the farthest corner of the stockroom, stood it upright, gathered up several empty, scattered boxes, and hid the large jug behind them.

Neo then noticed a gleam of metal bouncing off the dim light behind another pile of empty boxes in the stockroom. As she walked toward it, she bent down and swatted away other empty mangled boxes, using her right hand as a box windshield wiper. The metal that caught her eye belonged to a small college-dorm sized refrigerator. She could hear an occasional slight humming sound when the compressor motor kicked in.

She eagerly opened the refrigerator door and found a can of Spam, a plastic six-pack of mixed fruit, and on the door shelf was a fresh pound bag of beef jerky strips. She also found several sealed packages of chocolate-chip cookies, her favorite, and quickly reached for a lower compartment that contained fresh low-fat milk. She reasoned that at least she could enjoy a nice snack later, as frivolous as that seemed at the moment.

Convinced she hadn't missed anything else, Neo left the stockroom and headed back out to the front of the store. She placed everything she found, except the jug of water, in a small, fairly intact box she was able to dig out from the stockroom. She then loaded it all into a bright yellow plastic shopping basket from a stack located near the front door.

It wasn't much, but it was better than nothing at all, and more than enough to at least get her through the night, maybe even a couple of days. It would also afford her some time to devise a better plan, or hope the rescue team showed up. She knew she would have to venture out to one of the larger food stores soon to see if she could find a larger supply of food and other items, assuming the other stores hadn't been ransacked as well.

Another concern crept into Neo's thought process. She wasn't sure how long the power would keep running. As soon as the electricity stopped running, her water supply would disappear soon after, as would her heat during an occasional chilly Los Angeles late evening, and any means of cooking her food. It was highly important that she locate a bundle of water and anything she could consume out of a can since it's a nonperishable item that doesn't need to be cooked to be eaten.

Neo picked up her basket of goodies and headed to the exit. A second small refrigerator near the door hummed quietly to itself. She hadn't bothered to check it when she came in, certain it would be empty. As she passed it she stopped and pulled back the sliding glass top and took a peek inside. Jackpot. She scooped up a pint tub of Baskin-Robbins Oreo ice-cream. "You're coming home with me, baby," she said with a smile, and added it to the basket on her way out of the candy store.

Outside, full darkness had settled upon Los Angeles, but Neo could see the storm of colorful dust still swirling in the glare of the streetlights. It appeared to have gotten stronger and looked like a light snowfall from a colder east coast region.

She could barely make out the hazy shape of her apartment building across the street. The building's outdoor security lights created a beacon that she could acclimate herself by, but only scarcely. There was just enough light to see, and she feared the weird dust storm would only get worse.

Neo opened the door to the street. Specks of yellow-red dust rushed through the gap in the doorway and into the empty store, whirling around her. Within seconds, the small candy store was filled with a rush of small dust particles.

She stood her ground, her eyes blinking as waves of dust flew toward her, yet swerved around her, continuing into the store as if she didn't even exist. Bewildered, she watched the dust maneuver its way through the building. It seemed to be searching for something, but not finding what it was looking for. It then flowed back out through the doorway again, only to be replaced by more dust.

Neo raised her hand to push a lock of hair from her face. Strangely, as she moved her arm toward her forehead, the flow of dust navigated around it like the smoke in a wind tunnel blowing over a car, avoiding any attempted contact with her.

She wanted to see if what she was seeing was actually happening, so she tried the same movement with her other arm, then took a step backward. The dust particles shifted right along with her, but didn't touch her at all, leaving about an inch of space between her body and the crowd of swirling particles. It seemed as if the dust particles were avoiding her on purpose.

Neo's mind crept back to the scene of where the dead man lay in front of the candy store, and how the dust attached itself to his skin. Was the dust searching for the dead? The thought sent a chill through her body. How could that even be possible? There *had* to be another explanation. As she stood in the candy store doorway, she observed the endless stream of dust swirl around the room before suddenly leaving the store without even a hint of a breeze to propel it.

If she were correct in her assumption, then she was definitely observing something far more serious than a natural disaster or a chemical spill. At least those could log-ically explained, unlike this dust storm phenomenon. Neo wondered if perhaps there was some type of advanced in-telligence controlling the event, driving the dust to seek out the dead, which would mean it was of a synthetic nature, which terrified her even more.

Neo let out a sigh of dejection, lowered her head, and weaved below and around the flow of the colorful dust above and around her. She turned and picked up her small shopping basket from the floor, walked out of the candy store, and began the trek back to her apartment building across the street.

***

The stroll back to her apartment wasn't nearly as odd as she had expected. However, it was more difficult than she had expected. The swirling tide of dust made it nearly impossi-ble to see more than a few feet in front of her. It seemed as if she was walking through one of the worst January snow storms she had remembered while growing up in Montana.

The dust continued to keep its distance from Neo, whizzing past her as it thoroughly searched the streets for whatever only it knew. Neo was grateful that it seemed as though there was some sort of shield surrounding her, not al-lowing the dust to penetrate her immediate personal space.

Partially blinded by the dust storm all around her, she didn't anticipate the raised curb of the pavement as her right foot caught the top edge of it, sending her sprawling and nearly falling to the ground. Like a pro, she didn't spill not one item from her candy store basket full of goodies.

Minutes later, a frustrated and tired, Neo finally pushed the door open and stepped inside her apartment building lobby. She was welcomed home by the now familiar whirl of dust that had followed her inside before she was able to close the door behind her. The stream then suddenly scattered away from her.

She paused momentarily to take in a few deep breaths before she made the long climb up the stairs to her apartment on the seventh floor. Why not the elevator? Well, it still housed the dead body of the woman she had found on her floor, and she wasn't about to spend another second of time in the presence of dead people, if she could at all help it.

***

Neo stood at the perch at her window and gazed down upon the streets below. She had already put her candy items and ice-cream away, taking inventory of precisely how much food she had gathered coupled with the food she already had in the pantry.

There wasn't much when she added it all up. She guessed that she had two days' worth of food to live off of, and more than enough water to drink to last her at least a week, including the large jug of water she hid in the candy store stock room. If those supplies were to be consumed any sooner than a week, she knew she could always confiscate a vehicle on the street and drive to the local Wal-Mart for more rations.

Feeling dirty, sweaty, and grimy, she had decided to fill the bathtub with as much water as she could before she went to bed. She planned to use the water in the bathtub for bathing herself and washing her clothes. There was a laundry room on the third floor, but she didn't want to risk leaving her apartment any time soon. A decent water supply was vital to her survival.

Neo had no idea how long the purification process Los Angeles used to sanitize the water the city supplied to its residents would function as normal, or for how long without any human operation. It was safer for her to assume that the city's water would be compromised at any moment, meaning she could no longer drink water from the faucet after this evening.

She had no clue who or what was going on in the city or what toxins could have entered into the supply with several million dead people just lying around decomposing. It just wasn't worth the risk of drinking poisonous water when there was an abundance of bottled water available from local stores. The hot bath tonight was a welcomed, last extravagance; that and the Oreo ice-cream she retrieved from the freezer, before she resigned herself to being cautious about everything she would do going forward.

She slowly walked from the living room into her bathroom, turned on the bath's hot and cold faucets, filled the tub, threw in some much needed and soothing bath salts, stripped off her dirty clothes, grabbed the bucket of ice-cream, and stepped into the steaming hot bath. Neo soaked her aching body for nearly an hour.

By the time she hesitated in climbing out, disappointed that the bath had ended, her skin was all wrinkled like a kid who had stayed in the pool far too long. She didn't care about that minor reaction to the hot bath. She actually finally felt like human again. She knew it would be a long time before she could repeat the luxury of a hot bath and ice-cream.

She emptied the bathtub, cleaned off the ring of dirt that had accumulated around it, then refilled the tub with cold water while she toweled herself off. She slipped on her favorite purple flannel pajamas and strolled back into the living room.

The street below was barely noticeable as she stared at the darkness from her favorite perch at the window. The streetlights were almost invisible beneath the thick fog of dust that seemed to be growing larger by the second. She guessed that the same thing was happening throughout Los Angeles, perhaps the entire country, and maybe even the whole world.

This was an event so colossal, so utterly out of her control that it was completely liberating to know that there was not a damn thing she could do about it – except wait. All Neo had was time. She sat back and watched the show to see what might happen next, and hoped she could survive another day, or maybe longer.

She continued to watch the flow of the expanse of dust as it swelled through the streets of LA for nearly two hours before her eyelids became heavy. She yawned, pulled the drapes closed, and lumbered to her bedroom, closing the door on both the world...and the day.

OOZE

9

The Third Day

WHEN NEO WOKE UP she was ready to hit it and get it.

She popped her head out from under the covers and glanced at her bedside alarm clock. It revealed 7:48 A.M. in large white numerals. The bedroom felt warmer than usual; the air-conditioning should have come on by now. The power was still on because her alarm clock was working. Perhaps there was a problem with the thermostat.

She climbed out of her bed, pulled on her robe, walked into the living room, and emptied enough water in the coffeemaker to brew eight cups. She had a feeling that it was going to continue to be a long, strange day.

She had slept well, better than she could have imagined under the circumstances, and this was the first morning since the world fell apart that she actually felt *normal,* and clear minded enough that she could turn her thoughts back to figuring out how she was going to contact whoever was still alive. It was apparent from her efforts yesterday that calling locations that she thought might be the rational centers for an organized rescue wasn't going to work.

She couldn't be the only person left in the world; she was sure of that. The law of averages made it next to impossible for her to be the sole survivor. Today was going to be the day she figured out how she was going to make contact with human life.

The question burning in her mind as she walked over to the living room window, was how was she supposed to find other survivors when there were no clues as to who they were, their location, or whether there was even anyone alive to contact.

She reached out and drew back the drapes from the window. Outside her seventh-floor window was nothing but the same swirling horde of dust. It engulfed the entire skyline, blocking the view of everything for miles.

Below, she could barely see the dim glow of the streetlights, their light-detecting circuits faked out by the heavy swarm of yellow-red dust into thinking darkness had come early. The dust crept over the outside of the window like a swarm of bees protecting its honey.

Neo now wondered if the dust phenomenon was actually some type of an animal. She leaned closer to the window, trying to follow one of the particles as it tapped the pane of glass, but then it moved across the glass too quickly for her to follow and darted away before she could get a good look at it, only to be replaced by another, slightly larger particle.

In the few moments she was able to track the larger particle of dust, which was the size of a small marble. She could tell that it certainly didn't resemble any kind of bug she had ever seen before. It looked like normal dust, like one of those thick dust bunnies that collect for weeks under your bed or couch.

Actually, it looked more like plant pollen. It had an irregular curved shape with a sharp point sticking out at weird angles, but rather than looking solid, the particle she was staring at was see-through and almost as delicate as the dandelion's seeds she had seen floating in the wind in Montana when she was a kid.

It was impossible to tell how much of Los Angeles was held captive by the dust storm. If she wanted to find that out, she was going to have to venture away from her apartment. She hoped that it was just some kind of localized effect that had caused the dust to collect on her side of the building. The idea that this might be happening all over the city was discouraging. Neo unlatched the security lock on her apartment door and opened it. She stopped before she even set a foot outside the door.

Running along the ceiling just outside her door was a ringlet of the same dust. She poked her head outside the apartment doorway and scanned the hallway to the elevator. The dust curled and spiraled about an inch below the ceiling.

It seemed to be coming from the direction of the exit to the main stairwell. A few feet into the hallway, it split into two sections, with one ringlet heading toward the apartments to the right of the stairwell and the other inching its way in her direction.

Sections of the dust twisted down over the doors of each of the hallway's apartments as if it was pulled along by a breeze, yet there was none. As she watched, Neo saw a string of the dust break off from the main root and slide down to the door of Mrs. Jones' apartment two apartments down the hallway. The string cascaded over the doorway, the tip making small movements left and right as if was trying to feel its way around.

The dust ringlet vanished into the tiny keyhole opening as a second strand continued down to the base of the door. When it reached the floor, the second ringlet began to probe at the thin space between the base of the door and the floor, as it searched for another entrance into the apartment.

Neo slammed her door shut and sprinted to the linen closet. She flung the door open and snatched up a handful of the thickest towels she could find, then ran to the kitchen, nearly tripping as she rounded the corner. She threw the towels into the sink and turned on both faucets full force.

Sure that the towels were completely soaked, she raced to the front door and threw the dripping wet towels down onto the floor to block the crack, pushing them tightly into place as though she were trying to stop smoke from a fire.

The edge of the door where it met the door frame was secure, so she wasn't concerned that anything could get through that. The keyhole, however, was another problem. It was obviously too small to block with a towel, and she didn't want to plug it with wet paper because that would be a bitch to get out later. There was no way in hell she was going to risk not being able to lock her door, or worse, trapping herself inside.

Neo zipped back into the kitchen and began pulling out each of the drawers. She knew she had a roll of duct tape around somewhere. She found it and raced back to the front door. She tore off three three-inch strips and pressed the pieces over the keyhole just as the first few strands of dust began to float through the hole. She stood and watched in awe as the dust float away from the door toward her kitchen. She tore off a fourth piece of tape and stuck it diagonally across the other pieces she had already applied.

She stepped back from the door and inspected her work, taking talking care to look for any signs the dust may have found some other way through that she hadn't noticed. There was no sign that she had missed any gaps and, after an anxiety filled minute of double-checking, she breathed a sign of relief.

Neo then realized the air-conditioning had actually failed to kick-on this morning. Perhaps it was simply an electrical glitch. Her apartment building was installed with a central forced-air system which fed all of the apartments in the building. A couple of days with no human activity may have created an electrical malfunction, causing the unit to overload and shut down.

After witnessing the meticulous way the dust had searched out every possible entry point into the other apartments on her floor, Neo doubted it was anything as simple as an electrical or mechanical failure. The apartment's sudden noise was more likely caused by the strange dust, which had found its way into the central air-conditioning unit and overloaded it. It could now be making its way through hundreds of feet of ducts throughout the building, seeking a way into every crack or crevice in each of the 225 apartments.

Grabbing the roll of duct tape once again, Neo bolted back down the hallway to the living room. The vents were too high for her to reach, so she double-backed into the breakfast nook and grabbed a chair. A vent sat directly over the wooden table in the breakfast nook.

Neo climbed up onto the chair then stepped onto the table, hoping it wouldn't collapse under her weight. Thankfully, it didn't. The vent was closed, but she could still see a small gap between each of its oval fans that she was sure was more than large enough for the small particles of dust to wiggle its way through.

Two flathead screws held the vent in place. She could see a black line of shadow between the edges of the vent and the white paint of the ceiling. It meant that the vent casing didn't sit flush with the ceiling. She tore off strips of duct tape and stuck them over the exposed seams between the vent cover and the ceiling, fingering them into place to make sure it made a tight seal. She tore off a few more strips and stuck them across the panels, perfectly obscuring the vent. She was lucky that she had enough tape to cover all of her apartment's vents.

Twenty minutes later, she placed the last strip of tape against the vent in her bedroom. She was able to cover them all and, looking at the roll of tape she had, she was confident she had enough left for a few more strips to patch up anything she might have missed.

Her apartment was going to get hot in a hurry with no air-conditioning. She could already feel the temperature rising in her bedroom. At some point she would have to open a window and allow some fresh air. The timing of that event would depend on how long the dust would stick around.

Neo had managed to cover all of the possible ways into her apartment she could think of, and felt a bit more secure. The impressive intelligence that the dust had displayed to coordinate entry into all of the apartments in the building was, in her mind, proof that what she had seen over the past forty-eight hours was not a coincidental cluster of unrelated events. Instead, it was seemingly a part of a far larger phenomenon.

Whatever it was, Neo understood that something astronomical had been set in place with the fall of the ooze rain, and that it was slowly and systematically moving toward its final target – whatever that target was. That was still to be determined.

***

Checking the window periodically to see if the dust storm had subsided had tired Neo. Whenever she pulled the curtains aside and looked out, the dust storm seemed to only become stronger. It had gotten so thick that when she glanced toward the street, she couldn't tell if the streetlights had stopped working, or if the massive dust covering Los Angeles was so blinding that the light couldn't even be seen.

As the hours slowly passed by, Neo found herself pacing the floors of her apartment. She switched on the TV, and scanned each and every channel in hopes that a station, any station, anywhere, would be investigating and reporting on a post-phenomenon report that gave her a clue of what the initial ooze rain had caused, and whether there were any other survivors. Static was all she saw and heard on nearly every channel.

The internet was her next option. She yanked her laptop from her backpack and connected it to the modem she kept on a small desk next to her bed. She expected the internet would down as well, but much to her surprise and glee, she smiled when she saw the red connection indicator inform her that she was now connected after she plugged the Ethernet cable into the connecter.

Neo tried all of the major news sites first. CNN was still active, but it displayed the same headline it had the day before the ooze rain came down. The same held true for

CBS, NBC, ABC, Fox, and MSNBC. The sites were all functioning, but there was nothing new that had been reported.

She began working her way through the list of social media sites such as Twitter and Facebook, and blogs she had compiled the day before, searching for any hint that someone had tweeted or posted a message that they had made it through the ooze rain alive. There were only a few messages that dispelled the thought of a threat, calling it nothing more than frightened hysteria.

Neo typed in the message: "PLEASE HELP! I AM ALIVE!" on several social media sites. She also included the date and her cell phone number. She was reluctant to leave her address for security reasons, so she simply typed, "Los Angeles."

After exhausting her list of other websites, her eyes had begun to burn from the strain of staring at her laptop screen for such a long time. With the air-conditioning still not working, she felt beads of sweat rolling down her back and chest. Her apartment was in lock-down, which resulted in increasingly growing humidity.

Neo walked to the bathroom where the bathtub still held her emergency supply of water. This meant that she would have to drain it if she wanted to take a shower. She instead chose to fill the sink with water as she shed her clothing and rinsed herself off with a face towel. The cold water felt refreshing against her clammy skin. Afterward, she tossed on a fresh T-shirt and underwear, and felt a bit rejuvenated.

Neo's stomach was angrily growling at her to feed it, and *now*. She pulled a can of Chunky beef soup from her food stash and heated it on the stove, which unfortunately raised the temperature in her apartment even higher. She strolled to the sofa, sat down, and devoured the soup along with a few slices of wheat bread she had left. While she ate, she flipped the TV on again and found a movie channel that was still broadcasting old-fashioned horror movies.

Anxious, frustrated, and not able to focus, she switched the horror movie off before it ended because she was currently living a *horror* of her own. She lifted herself from the couch and walked over to the her favorite window to observe the weather outside. The dust was still tapping against the glass. Looking out, she couldn't tell if the dust storm had gotten worse or remained the same as before.

The ever increasing temperature in her apartment, along with the distress about her situation, sucked the energy out of her. Saddened, she realized that there was nothing much else she could do today. She needed to rest as it would do her no good to let worry consume her to the point of physical exhaustion. That would be no help to her cause at all. The heat in her apartment made it uncomfortable to even try and get comfortable. She reluctantly climbed into bed on top of the temporary, yet appreciated coolness of her comforter.

While she slept, the dust storm carried on outside her apartment window. It continued to bounce off the window glass, searching for a way to gain access.

OOZE

10

The Fourth Day

THE FAINT, UNMISTAKABLE sound of a baby crying woke Neo out of a deep sleep.

When the sound initially found its way to her ears, she thought she was dreaming as she tried to wake up from a sleep state of being. She was sweaty from the unrelenting heat while she slept overnight. Even the comforter that she lay spread-eagled diagonally across the bed was moist from her perspiration. She sat up in bed and tried to stand, but she became light-headed and wobbly.

Then, she heard the the sound again as she sat on the corner of her bed. It was the familiar cry of an actual *baby*. Neo's adrenaline suddenly kicked in. She jerked her body upright while she listened intently to to the sounds to ensure she wasn't just hearing a mechanical noise created by the building, or a neighbor's TV in an apartment nearby.

No...that was *definitely* a baby crying.

Bawagghhhhh!

The sound drifted to her again. It was the sound of something *alive*. The sound was distant, yet Neo could tell it was coming from inside the building from somewhere above her apartment. Perhaps the next floor up?

Bawagghhhhh!

The cry became louder, and she could tell that it did indeed seem as though it was coming from the floor directly above hers, maybe even the floor above that one. It didn't matter which floor it was coming from. She didn't have a second to lose before springing into action to save the baby.

She had spent all of her time searching for survivors. It never crossed her mind that there might be children still alive out there. A kid wouldn't understand the implications of a fire alarm. A baby surely couldn't let Neo know it was there, except by doing the one thing that a baby does instinctively when distressed – c*ry like hell.*

She figured that the baby had been on its own from day one of the ooze rain. It sounded young to Neo, perhaps no older than a year or so. She couldn't imagine what the poor baby had gone through the past few days, stranded in a room on its own. Its parents...likely dead. Neo would have to act quickly if she was going to rescue the child. She first needed to check on the ever present dust storm outside.

Convinced that the dust had no interest in her whatsoever, and her theory likely also extended to the baby, she didn't want to risk exposure to the dust any more than she already had. She knew she was dealing with an unknown entity.

She had no idea what the potential long-term effects of coming in contact with it would do her. Even with that thought, the future was the furthest thing from her mind at the moment. What was imperative now was locating and rescuing the crying baby as quickly and safely as possible.

She hopped off her bed with authority, slipped into a pair of jeans and a T-shirt, stumbled her way to the living room window, threw back the drapes, and was surprisingly greeted by a beautiful blue sky and with a view of Los Angeles that spread for blocks. There wasn't a single clue of even one speck of dust – just clear, blue skies.

Neo stood with her mouth wide open in amazement at the view outside her window. Not a particle of the dust could be seen, at least not from her seventh floor apartment. It was as if the dust storm she had experienced for the past couple of days decided it wasn't having any fun visiting Los Angeles and packed up its dust particles and left, like nothing ever happened.

Forget about *"what happens in Vegas stays in Vegas."* What had obviously happened the past two days and overnight in Los Angeles, definitely didn't *stay* in Los Angeles. Good riddance, she thought.

Wa...wagghhhhh!

The baby's cry jolted Neo from her thoughts. She instantly shifted her attention and excitement away from the newly dust-free sky to finding the baby.

Even though the view from her living room window served up clear, cloud-free skies, that didn't mean the dust entity wasn't still lurking somewhere inside her apartment building hoping to fake her out and engulf her when she walked out into the hallway.

Neo sped back to the bedroom, scooped up her sneakers from beside her bed, laced them up as fast as her fingers could, and darted to the front door. She then stopped in her tracks. She turned around and bolted to the hallway. She needed a blanket for the baby. She didn't know what baby had been exposed to the past couple of days. She had to be sure that she had a blanket to wrap the baby in when she brought it back to her apartment.

She rummaged through her linen closet and found the light green baby blanket that her Mom had sheathed her in when she was a child. She sprinted back to the front door and peered through the peephole out into the main hallway. Neo didn't see any evidence of the dust that was the cause of so much grief and despair the previous day and night.

The peephole allowed her only a limited view of the hallway, so she needed to proceed with caution. She understood that she had been in contact with both the ooze rain and the dust without any damage being done to her personally, but she knew that could change at any moment.

Her adrenaline was surging off the charts. She was deathly afraid to step outside of her apartment, yet she knew she had to save the baby. Which was stronger: *fear or courage?*

The towels at the bottom of her front door had long dried out due to the high humidity in her apartment. Instead of pulling them away, and ripping the tape from the keyhole, she decided to take only the towels away first, in case she needed to put them back right back into place.

With the towels removed, Neo slowly slid the security chain off its fastener, fingered the button on the door latch, and gave the door handle a gentle, careful twist. She felt a refreshing wave of cool air sweep over her face, blowing strands of her hair backward as she opened the door only a little bit. Thankfully, the air-conditioning had started once again.

Neo let the air cool her off for a moment as she peered through the small opening of the door that she created. She hurriedly scanned the hallway up and down, checking the ceiling first, then the floor. No signs of the dust was present.

She opened the door a bit more, her eyes searching the hallway for any movement. She was ready to slam that sucker shut at any hint of trouble. There was nothing. Fairly confident, she opened the door open wide enough to poke her head outside, so that she had a full view of the hallway in all directions.

The ridiculously peculiar dust that was so intent on clinging to every crevice of her apartment building and the city, had now been declared *MIA*. There seemed to be no sign of it anywhere, at least not on her floor. As she took a closer look, she noticed a fine yellow-red residue sprinkled over the floor of the hallway. It stood out against the dark, star and moon speckled carpeting.

It looked similar to the yellow-red dust, but it was more like a light orange color, and seemed to be devoid of the forces that had allowed it to float in the air so effortlessly. It appeared to be brittle to the touch, and granular. Whatever this residue was, it appeared brittle and grainy. It looked nothing like the super delicate dust form Neo had seen propelling through the air only two days earlier.

She stepped out of her apartment fully and quietly closed the door behind her as she listened for any clues of where the baby was. A minute or so later, she heard the baby's cry again. Its cries came through was louder in the hallway, allowing her a hint to its location. It was coming from either an apartment or the hallway above her. She took off running toward the stairwell.

Crunch!

The sound startled her and, as she gazed down at her feet, she saw that she had stepped on a chunk of the immobile dust, crushing it underneath her feet like crisp autumn foliage that had fallen to the ground. Neo lifted her right foot and noticed the crispy dust now turned into a fine powder.

Tiny nuggets of it stuck into the grooves on the sole of her sneaker. She wasn't sure what the significance of this was, but while she slept overnight, the dust had died. The powdered residue was all that was now left of it. *R.I.P dust.* You won't be missed, she thought, causing her to chuckle.

While continuing her quest to save the baby, she tried her best to ignore the constant crunching sound of the dust under her feet as she headed for the stairwell. She would high tail it up to the eighth floor first and listen for the baby there. If she couldn't find out where the cries were coming from, she was resigned to going door-to-door while listening.

A blast of scenarios raced through Neo's mind as she dashed up the flight of stairs. What if the baby wasn't the only survivor in its apartment? What if its parents were also still alive, or its siblings? That concept would logically explain how the baby had survived all of this time. She was excited at the thought of other human life and possible interaction.

For much of her life, Neo had been a loner. The fact that she chose a career that was based on constant contact with people, even asking them questions about their personal lives if that was warranted, had surprised both her parents and the few close friends that she had. The cool thing for her was that as a journalist, any contact and communication was always on *her* terms.

She dictated the beginning and end of her interaction with each person she interviewed and questioned, allowing her to maintain complete control of the amount of exposure she had with people. If and when she would become tired of talking with or interviewing them, she ended the interview – simple as that.

Neo began to call out as soon as she made it to the eighth floor. "Hello?" she yelled. "Can anyone hear me?"

She heard the baby cry again as if it heard her voice and answered her plea. The cry was much louder this time, and definitely somewhere on the seventh floor.

Wagghhhhh!

She froze in her stance for a moment to try and identify which direction the cry was coming from.

Wagghhhhh!

She was sure it came from her right side, and just a few doors down the hallway.

"Hello," she yelled out again. "Keep crying so I can find you!"

Wagghhhhh! Wagghhhhh!

A quickened sense of urgency now came in loud and clear from the baby's cries. Good thing, because Neo had actually passed the apartment door where the it was coming from the first time around. She turned and doubled back three apartments and stood outside the door of the apartment that she was thought the baby was in. She placed her hand flat against the wood of the door and gave it a good push. It was locked. She twice pounded the side of her fist against the door.

"I'm right outside your door," she yelled. "It's okay! I'm here to help you!"

Wagghhhhh!

Without a doubt, she knew she had the right apartment. It would be a near miracle if the baby had survived on its own. That was the past. This is the hear and now. She knew she was the baby's only hope of continued survival. There was one major problem. The door was locked shut and of course, she didn't have the key to unlock it.

She knew she didn't have the bulk or strength to kick the door in, even with all the years she spent as a youngster and older teen working on her parent's farm helping her Dad lift bails of hay, and help him transport small pieces of farm equipment and tools from one location to another.

Besides, what if she seriously hurt herself, or injured the baby if it were on the floor nearby? It required a more thoughtful, strategic plan to force the door open. Time was of the utmost essence.

Neo ran back to the stairwell after remembering something that she had noticed on her way to the eighth floor. A large, red fire extinguisher housed in its own container behind a pane of glass, was on the side of the wall. Next to it was a similar red box and behind it was large, red, long-handle fire hatchet.

A small metal hammer hung from a chain on the right side of the box. Neo grabbed the hammer, turned her head away, closed her eyes, and whacked the glass with all the force she could generate, shattering it. Fealing mighty proud of herself, she grabbed the ax with both hands, yanked it away from its restraining clasps, and ran back to the baby's apartment.

When she got back to the door, she paused to study it for a moment. She decided to demolish the door handle and lock instead of chopping holes in through the door large enough to reach an arm through to unlock it from the other side. The lock served as the path of least resistance in gaining entry into the apartment.

Wagghhhhh! Wagghhhhh!

"Hold on, little baby! I'm almost to you!"

She need some good force behind her swing and planted her feet shoulder-width apart with enough room between herself and the door. The hatchet weighed about twenty five pounds, causing her to stumble backward the first time she lifted it above her head for the first attempted swing at the door. Even with a stumble, she still felt like a *badass* with an attitude. She shifting her weight back and forth to balance herself while still holding the hatchet, and tried again. She heaved it up to her head and took dead aim at the lock chamber.

Neo took in a deep breath, reared the hatchet back without toppling backward, brought it down on the door lock behind every pound on her body. The first high impact strike resulted in nothing more than a partly damaged metal lock and a nicked up door knob.

She grunted in anger as the baby continued to cry. She hoisted the hatchet just above her head one more time and tried again. The second attempt resulted in the shattering of the metal shaft of the lock chamber into three sharp chucks and to the floor in opposite directions. One of the sharp pieces just barely missed hitting Neo in the face, but she quickly turned away just in time.

A small fourth piece of the lock dangled from the wood of the door. Neo freed a hand and dropped the head of the hatchet to the floor with a thud, careful not to chop her foot off in the process. She reached out with her other hand and wiggled the last piece of the lock free from its former casing. Huffing, she reached down, turned the door knob, and...*voilà!*

Wagghhhhh! Wagghhhhh!

After Neo turned the door knob without putting any weight against the door, it slowly opened under its own power. As the baby cried out once again, she wiped sweat beads away from her forehead and cautiously stepped inside the baby's apartment.

Something didn't seem right. She couldn't precisely pinpoint it, but she had a sudden strong sense that her attempt to rescue the baby was *not* going to be an easy task. The apartment was dark and creepy beyond the door. The baby cried out again. The sound was even louder because Neo was so close to him or her.

Wagghhhhh!

OOZE

11

THE STENCH OF AMMONIA hit Neo's nostrils as soon as she eased into the apartment. The smell was so strong it literally made her gag. It took her a full minute to fight back the urge to puke before she could even consider walking any further inside.

She was unexpectedly taken aback big time. The repulsive odor was worse than a hundred cats abandoned in a sealed apartment for a month. Waves upon waves of heat rolled out through the open door and past her as the stench itself seemed to be screaming during its escape.

Neo felt more rolls of sweat dripping from *everywhere*. She wondered if the baby's parents were hiding a dead body in there, in addition to the baby, and a hundred cats. She couldn't imagine how on earth a defenseless, helpless child could possibly have survived this long while breathing in the poisonous air.

If she would have known the smell was going to cause her to nearly pass out, she would have moistened one of the towels she put at the the bottom of her apartment door earlier to use as a filter against the ferocious ammonia that riddled the air in the baby's apartment. She had to make due with the end of her dangling T-shirt. She pulled it up and covered her nose and mouth while trying to fight back the burning tears that were stinging her eyes from the ammonia.

Within seconds of walking into the apartment, she was soaked with sweat and looked as if she had just taken a shower in her clothes.

Neo carried on. She wiped a pool of sweat off of her forehead, gritted her teeth, blinked hard twice to release the tears from her eyes, and stepped further into the apartment. She soon found a light switch and flipped it on. The overhead lights revealed an empty hallway with only a single painting hanging on the wall. The humidity was insufferable in addition to the ammonia.

"Hello?" she called out. She felt brave enough to remove her T-shirt cupped in her hand from her mouth and instantly regretted it, sucking in a large gulp of toxic air. She could feel it slowly scorching the roof of her mouth and the back of her throat, creating a painful chemical burn that she wouldn't wish upon her worst enemy. Neo tried to resist it all, but it was just too overwhelming.

She started coughing uncontrollably, then seconds later leaned over and sent a projectile of vomit onto the tan carpet. She ran out of the baby's apartment, slamming the door behind her, and back into the hallway gasping for air. Her lungs quickly welcomed the blast of fresh air. Dazed and disoriented, she stumbled against the wall, turned and rammed her back against it, and slowly slid down into a sitting position on the floor.

Neo took a good minute of catching her breath, she wiped the barf residue from her mouth with her T-shirt and tried to stand again. Her legs were weak, causing her to plop back down in a sitting position again. After taking in several deep breaths, she again tried to stand. This time, she had success. Still clutching her baby blanket in her hand she jogged to the stairwell again and began walking down the stairs back to her own apartment on the seventh floor.

When she got back to her apartment, her hands were still shaking as she fumbled with the keys to unlock the door. Once inside she grabbed both of the towels that she had put at the bottom of the door and headed to the bathroom. There, she submerged them each into the water-filled tub, pulled them out, then strong-armed the excess water from them into the basin.

She would use one of the now dampened towels to wrap completely around her nose and mouth, and the other one to tie around her head in an effort to keep her head from exploding from the wretched heat in the baby's apartment.

Finished wrapping herself up from the neck up, she took a glance in the bathroom mirror to study her handiwork. She looked like a mummy with her head and face completely covered, and each of her eyes barely exposed. Satisfied, she sprinted back out of her apartment, locked the door behind her, and it was back up the stairs to the eighth floor for round two of Neo vs. God forsaken stench of Satan.

Wagghhhhh!

She was going to save that poor baby – even if her *life* depended on it.

***

The ammonia wasn't nearly as biting to her eyes the second time around. She breathed easier, too. The smell was still repulsive, yet no longer vomit inducing. With a clearer mind, Neo noticed the baby's apartment floorplan was the next model up from hers. It had the same basic layout, but this one came had a second bedroom.

Common sense told her that the parents would have put the baby in the smaller second bedroom. She headed in that direction and pushed the door open while groping the wall for a light switch. She flipped the switch on and the light revealed what she she had thought – a nursery. A cute crib sat against the right wall, and dangling from the ceiling above it was a baby's activity play set.

Large purple and gold animals hung from the main frame of the toy. Pink wallpaper, decorated with colorful Disney cartoon characters, covered the room's walls. Across the door, Neo could see a changing station, and a high-back chair where the parents could sit and rock the baby or play with her on the floor. She walked over to the crib and pulled back the expensive-looking wool blanket. There was no baby beneath it.

Glancing around the room, Neo suddenly heard another cry echo in the room. Instead of immediately running toward the source of the cry, she stopped in her tracks. Her instinct again told her that something just didn't feel right.

Wagghhhhh!

The cry came again, more powerful. She realized, now that she was so much closer to the baby girl, that she could hear an odd quiver to her voice that made it seem far more complicated than the simple cry of a baby. It sounded...*creepy*. After listening intently for good minute, she realized the sound was mechanically generated. It actually now sounded less like a baby now that she could hear it clearly and was closer to it, without the layers of flooring, carpeting, and walls to filter it.

Neo tried to use logic and wondered if the strange vibrato to the cry she heard could simply be the result of the baby being abandoned in this noxious room for so long. She also had the urge to quietly leave the apartment and never come back. However, as strongly as her instincts might be telling her to leave, she couldn't. She *had* to find out what was making that noise, and whether it was a real baby or not.

She walked out of the nursery and crept toward the master bedroom directly across the hallway. She gently pushed the door open with the tip of her sneaker and reached inside for the light switch. She poked her mummified head in and quickly scanned the room. She saw a king-size bed that was neatly made and waiting for sleepers who would never again lay their heads down on those pillows. A bookcase filled with hardcovers was nearby, along with a night stand, but there was no sign of life inside the apartment, including the baby.

Neo turned and made her way down the hallway into the direction of the direction of the kitchen and living areas. The curtains were drawn closed, filling the living room with doom. With every step she took, she felt the temperature rising and the strong odor of urine become stronger. Although the area was darkened, she had a sense that something had moved, perhaps it was a shadow in the living room, causing her to catch her breath in fear.

Panic filled her heart and mind as she walked nervously through the apartment. Should she just forget about the baby and get the hell out of there, or stay? Why wasn't the baby crying anymore? Her strong investigative journalistic instincts and her overwhelming desire to rescue the baby, if there really was a baby, overrode her sense of self-preservation yet again.

Neo began blindly running her hand along the wall searching for the switch that would turn on the living room's overhead lights. The surface of the wall was sticky like dried up syrup. The light switch that she eventually found was much too high for a baby to reach. If it wasn't a syrupy substance, did someone throw up on the side of the wall? It was a mystery she wasn't interested in solving at the moment, or at any other time. She found the light switch and with a quick flip, lights filled the room.

It only took a few seconds for her eyes to adjust to the brightness. When she finally stopped squinting and batting her eyelids, she promptly started screaming.

It was as if she had turned a spot light directly onto the center of hell. Covering what had likely been the family couch, in the middle of the room looked like a gruesome scene straight out of *Dawn of the Dead*. What Neo was shocked beyond imagination to be viewing was the smorgasbord-style combination of cat-urine, coupled with the apartment's smothering humidity, with a baby – yes, *the* baby, added in for good measure.

There *was* a baby, or at least Neo imagined that it must have been a child at some point. The baby's parents were with it as well. The three family members had morphed into a single mass of fat, tissue, and other body parts.

The lower portion of the baby's body had seemed to disappear, contained in the pulsating bulk of the mass. Its torso and one hand were still free and visible. The hand moved lamely back and forth, almost as if it was waving at Neo.

The baby had no eyes. They were *gone,* replaced only by empty black sockets like some type of possessed doll. All along, the disturbing cries for help had been coming from this mutated...*thing.* While Neo stared at it in sheer horror, the baby, if you want to call it that now, opened its mouth wide and the familiar ear-piercing sound of its cry spilled out, filling her ears.

Wagghhhhh!

The baby girl's parents were hardly recognizable within the pulsating lump of largeness. If it weren't for the disconnected foot with the father's shoe still attached to it that lay a few feet away, and an obvious female arm that dangled from the left side, Neo wouldn't have known that the bodies were even human.

Thick blobs of yellow ooze moved over the skin of the mass in real time, pulling pieces of the main body with them and then moving them to other parts, almost as if it were putting together a puzzle. As Neo watched the ghastly reconfiguration, her mind was only a single thought from admitting she had gone completely insane from watching the sheer monstrosity before her.

It got worse.

A large glob of the yellow ooze left the altered body and reached out for the father's severed foot. It skillfully surrounded it, shoe and all, and began slowly moving it back to the main body.

What Neo was witnessing couldn't realistically exist. It was humanly impossible. She continued to watch in terrified shock as the foot was dragged back to the main mass, and the baby's head began a gradual clockwise rotation like Linda Blair's character, Regan McNeil, in the original *Exorcist* horror movie.

The baby's eyeless sockets stared at Neo from where its chin should have been. Its mouth opened wide and let out a long piercing wail that echoed throughout the apartment, bouncing off the walls and slicing through her brain with the precision of a surgeon's scalpel.

Wagghhhhh!

Neo's courage finally drained out of her body. She no longer gave a shit about the baby. All she could do now was scream and run the hell out of the apartment.

***

On her way out of the house of horrors, Neo's feet slid out from under her in the hallway as she rounded the corner from the front door while heading back to the stairwell. She toppled over hard, and knocked the wind out of her lungs. She quickly got back to her feet, arms flailing, and continued her Olympian-style mad dash back down the stairs to the safety of her own apartment.

She shouldered the door open leading from the stairwell onto her seventh floor hallway so hard, like a running back blasting through a defensive line in the NFL, it slammed back against its hinges, the aluminum handle taking a chunk out of the wall.

Still racing toward her apartment, she fingered the door keys from her jeans pocket. Her hand was trembling so badly that it took several attempts to put the key into the lock. The key suddenly seemed larger than life compared to the small slot that she tried to steady her right hand with to make the connection.

Finally, the key found its mark and the door opened. She bolted inside, huffing and puffing, then once inside, slammed the door shut behind her with a thundering *boom*.

She fumbled the security chain into place, quickly followed by the thumb lock, and ran down the hallway.

As her brain finally took back control of her body, she found herself standing in her bedroom, leaning firmly against the door. At that moment, the full, grotesque truth came flooding back to her. She understood why she was bracing her bedroom door closed. It was because something directly above her apartment should not, *could* not, possibly exist. Yet, it did. Neo's eyes drifted to the bedroom's ceiling. That *thing* was up there – right above her head.

What if that monster family upstairs was able to get out of the room? Were there more of them out there? What the fuck was she supposed to do about it? What if she, Neopolitina Marie Kao, really was the last human being left on earth, the sole surviving woman in a world full of mutated freaks? What if she *was* completely alone now?

It was at that moment, with so many questions flying around her brain, that Neo heard her cell phone ringing on the table in the living room.

OOZE

12

I'LL CALL THEM BACK LATER, Neo thought as her mind was still trying to grasp what had just happened. *They can leave a message.*

The fog obstructing her view of reality lifted on the third ring from her cell phone. She was out of the bedroom and halfway to the living room before it registered in her brain that she was in motion. She grabbed her phone from the table, tapped he answer tab on the screen, and pressed it to her ear.

There was nothing but silence on the other end of the call.

"Hello?" she whispered, her voice barely audible. "Please, somebody talk to me, *please.*" The silence continued for a moment longer until she heard someone take in a deep breath and a woman's voice broke through the silence.

"Is this Neo Kao?"

The smooth resonance of the stranger's voice in her ear had a soothing and reassuring effect on Neo. She felt as though she had received a call directly from the President of the United States.

"Yes, this Neo," she managed to say before she broke into a flood of tears.

"It's okay. Everything it all right," the woman's voice on the other end said softly. "You're not alone."

At that moment, a rush of numerous emotions swept through Neo. Relief, happiness, gratitude, fear, sorrow, all simultaneously took control of her body. Greater than all of those emotions combined, was an overwhelming sense of hope.

The flood of feelings caused her to stutter so badly that she couldn't respond to the woman's questions other than a weak yes or no answer. Attempting to articulate anything beyond that was pointless. The moment Neo tried to speak, she dissolved into a huffing bout of uncontrollable tears.

She allowed the relief to whisk her fears away in knowing she was not the only person who survived the ooze rain. At last, as she began to compose herself, she found the coordination in her tongue and began answering the questions more thoroughly that her caller was patiently asking.

The woman told Neo her name was Renee Miller. There seven other people with her, four men and three women in total. They were a team of scientists, technicians, and support staff working at a remote climate-monitoring station in Grand Forks, North Dakota.

Their group was, at least until the ooze rain came, a research team from the University of North Dakota Climate Research Center in Grand Forks, and that they had been stationed there for just over six months, gathering climatological data as part of a semiannual study.

Renee explained that no ooze rain had fallen anywhere near their base in Grand Forks, but that her husband, Andrew, who was stationed a few hundred miles south of his team's location back at the University of North Dakota, had reported that the phenomenon had been widespread. Renee became silent for a moment at the mention of her husband. Neo listened intently as light static buzzed in her ear. She wasn't sure if Renee was still on the line or not.

Seconds later, Neo spoke quietly into the phone. "Renee, are you still there?"

"Yes," Renee replied, just as quietly. Neo could hear her pain resonate in her voice. Renee was carrying a burden of loss as great as any Neo was feeling over the death of her parents, boyfriend, friends, and colleagues.

"We had a TV satellite feed, so we were following what was happening throughout Europe after the ooze rain had fallen," Renee continued. "Miranda said ooze had fallen all around the university; not much, just a smattering, but that I shouldn't worry because she hadn't been in contact with it. The university was going into lockdown and they were quarantining everyone who had any contact with the ooze rain, as best they could.

"Miranda told me she had managed to contact a few other weather and climate-monitoring stations scattered south of her and across the border in Ontario. They all reported significantly less amounts of the ooze rain the farther north they were. Eight hours after I last spoke with my husband, I tried calling him again on the shortwave, but he didn't answer. *No one* answered."

Renee whispered the last sentence between a barely restrained sob. The climatologist paused again as she collected herself before continuing.

"We have gotten reports of massive abandonment of posts already. Media stations in France and China are on it. Daycare centers, schools, hospitals, radar and traffic towers, police stations, utility plants – they're all shut down," Renee informed her.

"We also have a couple of satellite phones, so we all took turns calling family, friends, and colleagues at other research locations around the world. We called everyone that we could think of, but again, no one answered. Since then, our technicians have been scouring all the major websites and listening on the shortwave, trying to find someone, anyone, who is still alive. That's how we found, you, Neo. We're so happy to hear your voice."

Renee explained to Neo that no one on her team had come up with a solid theory for what exactly had happened, and were only speculating at best. They were, for the most part, clueless. One thing did seem obvious to the team of scientists was that from the data they had managed to collect before losing contact, the ooze rain phenomena covered a significant portion of the globe, and in Renee's opinion, it seemed to be a directed action against the most populated areas of the planet. As far as they could tell, not one country was left unaffected. There was not a major city, town, village, or precinct anywhere that had not been wiped out.

Neo was the first person her team had made contact with. They had picked up a few fleeting messages on the camp's shortwave receiver, but the signals had been too weak and too garbled to make any sense of, but it was a good indication, Renee said, that others had survived the disaster, somewhere.

"Of course, logic would dictate that there *must* still be pockets of survivors out there, likely small groups like us who live in the colder regions. Perhaps there are some military installations left. I suspect submarine crews are the most likely to have been unaffected by all of this, but who knows what will happen to them when they surface," Renee explained.

"What about your team?" Neo asked her. "What's your take on why all of you survived?"

"There's no way for us to understand whether this phenomenon is virus based, a nerve agent, chemical warfare, biological, or something else entirely. We're guessing that, for some reason, whatever kind of agent the ooze rain is, its ability to multiply and spread is affected by the cold, which is why my husband reported so little of it in Grand Forks and the other stations north of him.

"It appears that even minimum exposure to the rain proves fatal. Unless we can contact other survivors in colder areas across the globe we won't be able to confirm that hypothesis. For all we know, the moment we step foot inside the contamination zone, we'll drop dead. The same could happen to any other survivors outside the areas where the ooze rain fell."

Neo listened carefully to everything Renee had to say, but in the back of her mind she found herself wondering whether she should mention what she had experienced first hand with the ooze rain storm, or the thing impersonating a baby that she had seen in her apartment building.

Would Renee think she was crazy? If Neo were in her shoes, she sure as hell would. Telling Renee she had seen some kind of a monster made up of the young family that once lived in her apartment building wasn't exactly going to lend any kind of credibility to her story.

"I saw something, Renee," Neo told her, before she even knew she had made up her mind. "Something really creepy and definitely not normal."

Renee stopped mid-sentence. "What do you mean 'not normal,' Neo?"

"There's other horrible things that happened after everyone died. The ooze rain turned into some sort of bizarre dust and..." she paused, took a deep breath, then she uttered, "something is happening to the family in the apartment on the floor above me. They're dead but...they're...morphing into something else."

"Ooo-kaaay," Renee said, her voice taking on a baffled tone.

"Look," Neo continued, "I know it sounds completely insane. I know you're probably going to think I have lost my mind. I mean, I'm questioning my own sanity right now, but I promise I'm not making up what I'm about to tell you."

Neo told Renee about the yellow-red dust storm she had seen, how it had seemed to be attracted to the dead man in front of the candy store and then later attempted to invade her apartment, or how the dust didn't seem to want to come in contact with or harm her.

She thought to skip over how she had heard what she thought was a baby crying, tracked it down to the floor above, broke down the door, and found the baby monster inside, but the truth was, everything she had already told Renee sounded crazier than crazy anyway, so why not let it all hang out?

When Neo finished recounting her story, she waited to here the click of the phone as Renee hung up. She could imagine her wondering how the hell she had managed to connect with the last psycho person alive in Los Angeles.

"Interesting," Renee responded.

"You believe me?" Neo asked, still not sure what to think. "I'm *not* crazy, I swear."

"I can't speak to what you've experienced since the ooze rain, Neo. I believe we both know that if you had told me the same story before everything that's happened over the past few days, my response would probably have been different. Yet, after what you...what we have *all* experienced, I wouldn't discount any evidence that it's true, no matter how subjective it may be."

There was a few moments of silence between the two women, as both strangers contemplated what to say next. Finally, Renee spoke again.

"As I said before, we really only have assumptions to work with, but we've had little else to do around here other than run theories past each other. We have pretty much exhausted every possibility we could think of as a group, no matter how far-fetched it might seem, and we eliminated the majority of them as either impossible or highly unlikely."

Neo heard Renee take a drink of something, swallow, and then continue on with her theory.

"What we *are* certain of," she said, "is that something far outside the realm of probability has happened all around the world. Something so unnatural that it might just as well be defined as a random event because it's so damn far off the scale of reality.

"When we include the new data that you have supplied to us, it removes the possibility of the ooze rain being a man made event. There's no way human technology could have the kind of rapid effect on a human body that you just described as morphing, which means we're back to the drawing board in regard to trying to define what this is.

"If we rule out man-made technology, then we're left with the only two probable causes for the ooze rain and what you witnessed. The first is that it's a part of the natural cycle of the earth, a destruction-level event. There's plenty of data to suggest mass destruction happens, on a regular planetary timescale.

"We're long overdue for the next one. Perhaps the ooze rain is part of a cycle that kicks in every few hundred million years or so, wiping out the planet as we know it. What's really got me baffled is that the delivery of this event is so unexpected. It just doesn't seem possible that we would have missed some kind of evidence of it in our fossil records."

"What's the second probability?" Neo in asked, not sure she really wanted to know the answer.

"Well, again," Renee said, "call me crazy, but the only other possibility we can come up with is that this is some kind of extraterrestrial event."

Neo was shocked. "What? You mean like an alien invasion or something?"

"Yes, well, sort of. It depends on your definition of 'invasion.' What we could be experiencing here is a kind of extraterrestrial biological entity. Our plant is a massive super-organism. The ooze rain could be the equivalent of a virus, but one that exists out there in the expanse of space and affects planets instead of individuals, which in turn eventually affects the weather."

Neo could imagine Renee enthusiastically waving her hands toward the roof of her office all two-thousand miles or so away from her.

"The virus floats around until it randomly locks onto a suitable host planet and then mass destruction is the imminent result. The theory is compelling when you view it from a neutral frame of mind," Renee explained.

Renee realized that getting excited over the possible reason for the nearly total annihilation of humanity might not seem quite so attractive to anyone else outside of her small group of colleagues.

"I'm sorry, Neo," she apologized. I didn't mean to sound so exuberant about it all. That's what happens when you spend way too much time locked up with scientists twenty-four hours a day for months at a time."

"It's okay," she told her. "I understood what you meant."

"So, that's just two of the prime suspects we came up with," Renee continued.

"We simply don't yet know the real cause of what happened. I'm not sure if we'll ever know. However, we are fairly certain that something unprecedented in the entirety of human history has occurred, and all the old rules have been thrown out of the window. If we factor in your encounter, Neo, then the logical conclusion would seem to be that something far greater than a simple random cataclysm is at fault her. Which means that this is much more complex than we can even begin to imagine."

There was a long pause, then Renee's voice filled her ear again, crackling with static. "What are your plans now, Neo? How are you going to get out of Los Angeles?"

Renee's question caught her off guard. "What? I'm not planning on leaving my apartment, let alone Los Angeles. Why would I need to get out of the city?"

The earlier excitement she had heard in Renee's voice disappeared, replaced by a quieter tone.

"There's a lot of good reasons why you need to get out of LA as soon as possible. First of all, you're surrounded by several million dead bodies that are already well on their way to decomposing. At some point, that's going to bring you into contact with who knows how many potentially fatal pathogens, namely cholera, typhus, and others. It's all going to be floating around out there, and it's certainly not going to be a healthy place for you to live and breathe."

Renee hesitated before continuing, but when she did, Neo could sense her words tipped the scales of extreme life or death circumstances.

"If you're right about what you saw, then who's to say it's not happening everywhere? It's not my intention to frighten you, Neo, but maybe we need to consider that this event will have even further-reaching effects than we've imagined thus far. I hear myself say the words and I know how ridiculous I sound to you, but you have to consider that the transmutation you saw with the family might be happening all over the place. If it is, then we're talking about an unprecedented shift in the biological hierarchy of this planet, and to be quite honest, that scares the shit out of me."

"That's just..." Neo began to answer, but Renee cut her off, her voice insistent.

"Either way, you need to get out of there, Neo. If I were you, I'd be heading north, like right now."

"So what am I supposed to do? I'm pretty sure you guys aren't going to volunteer to come and pick me up, right? How do I get out of here and where am I supposed to go?"

Neo could hear the desperation in her own voice.

"How do you get out of Los Angeles? That I can't help you with, but where you need to go, that is simple. You need to head as far north as you can, or find a suitable vehicle left abandoned in the street and drive to us here in North Dakota. We're not going anywhere. The cooler it gets as you head north, the better your chances of continued survival. You have to be prepared, and you have to move – *now.*"

From upstairs, Neo heard the cry of the baby *thing* in the apartment. The idea that there could be more of them all around her, created the perfect sense urgency she needed to forge a plan to leave Los Angeles as Renee had strongly suggested.

"Okay," Neo said before she even realized that she had consciously made the decision to leave. "Tell me what I need to know."

"First things first," Renee told her. "The power isn't going to stay on forever, and we need to make sure you have some way to stay in contact with us. Do you know where you can get your hands on a satellite phone?"

Actually, Neo did know. The *Times* had a pair of satellite phones that they handed out to correspondents covering foreign events who had to travel to remote areas where regular cell phone coverage was either poor or nonexistent. The *Times* had put all their reporters through a three-hour-long training course when they had first purchased the phones.

Neo even had a chance to make a few calls, so she knew how to operate one. The phones were state of the art, and even came with a small 12-watt portable solar panel that could be set up in a couple of minutes and used to charge the battery when there was no access to a regular power source.

"Excellent," Renee said when Neo told her about the phones. Renee gave her the number to their satellite phone. "Just in case things begin to shut down faster than we anticipated," she said.

"I'll find a car on the street, hopefully one with the keys still in the ignition, and head over to the *Times* once we're finished talking. Wish me luck that nobody was using the phones when all of this ooze shit started hitting the fan."

The difficult part wasn't going to be finding a vehicle with the keys still in the ignition, or even getting out of Los Angeles, Renee explained. There was about two-thousand miles between Los Angeles and Grand Forks, North Dakota. That meant a full day and then some of driving. Then Neo would have to navigate her way to Renee's team in a remote location.

"Don't worry about trying to find us once you get to the university," Renee informed her. "We can come and get you once you make it there. What's imperative now is that we get you out of Los Angeles while this phenomenon is still in its early stages. We can formulate a better plan once we know you're safe and here with us."

The two women talked for another hour, exploring plans and ideas for the best course of action to get her on her way. Eventually the conversation turned to personal protection, and the need to defend herself.

"We don't completely know what all is out there, Neo. You need a weapon to protect yourself. Do you know where you can get your hands on a gun? If so, do you know how to use it?"

Neo's mind instantly flashed back to Nick. His service revolver had still been in its holster when she dragged his body into the apartment down the hall. She mentally kicked herself for not grabbing the gun when she had a chance to, but she reminded herself that she had other pressing matters on her mind at that time. How was she supposed to have known that she would even need a gun? She had been certain help was going to be on its way.

No one in their right mind would have guessed she would need to defend herself against some freak of nature consisting of a dead baby monster and its parents. What if what she had witnessed upstairs was also happening to her dead boyfriend as well?

Did she really think she could deal with that? No way was she going to try to get back into that room where she had left Nick. She would worry about finding a gun later, and hoped one would be conveniently located under a seat, in the glove compartment, a storage console of whatever car or truck she could find, or simply, at Wal-Mart, so that she could begin the long drive to North Dakota.

"I'm going to get off this phone if I need to get to the *Times* and back again before it gets dark," she told Renee.

"No problem. You have the email and the satellite phone if you need us. Remember, Neo, you're not alone. You can call us anytime while you're on the road to North Dakota. One of us will always be available to speak to you, got it?"

"Got it," Neo replied. The idea of hanging up, of severing the only connection she had been fortunate to have with anyone for the past several days was excruciatingly difficult to do. Renee must have sensed that.

"Neo, don't worry. Everything is going to be okay, I promise you. We'll touch base again soon. Call one of us every three hours of your drive to let us know how you're doing and that you're safe. Best wishes, and do be extra careful."

Before Renee hung up, she left Neo with one last piece of advice.

"Make sure you thoroughly check around the vehicle you're going to be driving, especially the interior. Try not to choose one that has any dead bodies inside, if you know what I mean."

Renee had tried to instill a bit of humor in her words in hopes of making Neo smile and relax a bit so that she can think clearly from this point forward.

"Thanks for the tip," Neo said with a chuckle. Renee then hung up, leaving nothing but dead air between them, and leaving Neo staring at a voiceless phone.

OOZE

13

NEO TAPPED AN ICON on the screen of her cell phone to officially end the call and glanced at the clock on the stove. It was 1:30 P.M. west coast time. That would allow give her about seven-hours of sunlight, which would give her plenty of time to find a vehicle and drive to the *Times* offices and return home before sunset.

The former reporter walked into the closet in her bedroom, raised herself on her tiptoes, and began feeling around on the top shelf. Eventually, her fingers found what she was searching for. She pulled out a large military-style backpack with numerous extra-large storage pockets, a gift from Nick back when they had taken a weekend camping trip at Lake Casitas in Santa Barbara. Nick had bought the backpack from a military surplus store in Hollywood. It had rained the whole time at the lake that weekend, but that hadn't mattered. It had been a great time, and she smiled at the memory.

She shook her head to rid herself of the pensive mood that sneaked upon her. The backpack would be useful because if she was going to make the drive to the *Times,* it would smart to make a stop at Wal-Mart and grab some supplies for an unknown future.

Before she grabbed her jacket and headed to the front door, a thought made her freeze in her stance. She turned and walked back to the kitchen and pulled out a ten-inch long butcher's knife from the cupboard. She didn't know if it would be of any use against the thing upstairs, or its relatives, but as she studied the sharp blade before slipping it into her backpack, it gave her confidence. She zipped up her backpack, swung it over her shoulder, opened the door, and warily walked out into the hallway.

The hallway was empty. As she quietly walked along, the sound of something shuffling on the floor above her made her stop in her tracks. It was a spooky, rumbling sound, as if a dead body was being dragged across the floor. Neo paused a second time, her heart beating emphatically in her ears.

She slowly lowered her backpack to the floor, knelt down, unlatched its two buckles, and pulled out the butcher's knife. She hadn't thought she would be putting it to use this soon, but whatever. She waited to see if the sound came around, but it didn't. Instead of putting the knife back into her backpack, she decided to carry it in her hand the rest of the way out of the apartment building, and beyond.

Safely outside her building, Renee's words echoed in her mind. *Get out of Los Angeles.* The closest thing to a human being was nearly two-thousand miles away. If the thing upstairs was flopping around, how long would it be before it, or its dead family members, decided to leave their rotting *home sweet home* and explore the rest of the building? What if the mutated baby monster and its posse was already wandering the hallways upstairs? Neo shuttered at the thought as she stood on the sidewalk.

Neo carefully studied the rows of abandoned vehicles in each direction on the street. She need one that was ultra reliable for the long drive to North Dakota, and still had the keys in the ignition. After all she had been through, if she could also find one that was stylish, she wouldn't hesitate to take it, and why not? She just hoped their wouldn't be any dead bodies inside of it.

If the vehicle she chose happened to break down during the drive to North Dakota, she was sure she would be able to confiscate any other vehicle of her choosing, knowing that the owner was most likely already dead. Neo remembered Renee telling her that the drive from Los Angeles to North Dakota was approximately 1,859 miles. That meant it would take a day and several hours to get there.

Neo walked up and down the street, peering inside car windows, opening car doors to check for keys in the ignition, which most of them had, and inspecting the exteriors as if she was a prospective buyer on a car dealership lot. Most of the abandoned vehicles showcased their mileage scars and other imperfections from years of road wars. Then Neo suddenly stopped walking when a particular vehicle caught her eye.

It was a beautiful newer model, candy apple red two-door Mercedes-Benz CL600 Coupe. She found what she was looking for. *"Vroom! Vroom!"* she smiled and whispered to herself. She inspected the exterior body of the car. It had not a scratch or dent on it. The doors were unlocked with the keys still in the ignition. She opened the door and the first thing she noticed was the pleasant aroma from an obvious air freshener, but it wasn't one of those cheap string cardboard-scented, rear-view mirror air fresheners.

Perfect, she thought.

The second thing she noticed about the Mercedes was that it was loaded with extra accessories such as burl wood molding, genuine leather seats, sun roof, advanced stereo and audio with CD player, and a GPS system, among other goodies. She triple-checked the interior to make sure it was safe before hopping into the driver's seat.

She pulled the keys from the ignition and studied them, trying to get a sense of the person who drove it last. There was nothing distinguishable about the key chain, just the usual lineup of car keys, house keys, and a couple of other, smaller, keys.

It was a sad moment for Neo. She knew that only days ago a man or woman had likely happily been driving along the street, perhaps listening to a favorite song on the radio and bobbing their head to the beat of the music, without a care in the world, and then... *BAM!*... the ooze rain came and ruined everything.

She wondered if the driver was male because she had to scoot the power seat forward *a lot.* Then again, during her time living in Los Angeles, she had spoken with, interviewed, and worked with quite a few tall women.

When she started it up, the Mercedes purred smoothly. A glance at the fuel indicator showed a little more than half-a-tank. She knew she would have no problems filling the tank during the drive to North Dakota. She could choose any gas station she pleased along the way.

***

There was no sign of the yellow-red dust storm from the previous day, only a few drifts of the same granular-like residue lined along exterior building walls and collected in the entryways of the shops and offices she passed as she drove toward the *Times* offices.

She drove past a ton of other abandoned vehicles, all of them void of drivers and passengers, as far as she could tell. In fact, during the entire drive she didn't see a single dead body. Even the dead birds that had littered the streets and sidewalks mysteriously disappeared.

Neo wondered what had happened to the dust. It didn't just walk away. Was there a more sinister explanation for the lack of dead bodies on the streets? She didn't want to think too deeply about it and become overwhelmed again. She forced her mind to do a U-turn and focus her thoughts back to driving to the *Times*. As she drove through the deserted streets of Los Angeles, she began recalling plans she and Renee had discussed during their phone conversation.

She would need supplies, fresh water, and nonperishable food. The farther north she traveled, the colder it was going to become, so she would also need to find a suitable wardrobe, such as warm clothes, boots, a heavy-duty insulated sleeping bag, and even snowshoes or skies.

She didn't think she would have much of a problem finding shelter on her drive north as there would be an abundance of vacant buildings between LA and North Dakota that she could use to sleep in for the night if necessary.

She pulled the Mercedes to the the front of the *Times* building and parked along the sidewalk. Instinctively, she pushed the security-lock button on the key chain, which triggered the quick horn-type *beep* letting her know the car was locked. She chuckled at why she did that because it wasn't as if someone would come by and steal it.

The front doors to the *L.A. Times* offices were obviously unlocked as the ooze rain struck during regular business hours. She pushed through a set of double doors and stepped into the deserted lobby area. A musty smell welcomed her. It smelled as if it had been deserted for years, like a large, abandoned library.

Neo came to the gloomy conclusion that there wouldn't be any news coming out of this building ever again. That realization brought tears to her eyes. The *Times* had been her life for nearly ten years. Up to this point, she hadn't given much thought to the fact that her journalism career was... *over.*

The pain of that reality was felt just as deeply as was the loss of her family and friends. Without the *Times,* and other newspapers big and small, who would write this world's obituary? If Neo were to write it, who on earth would be around to read it? Exactly. No one, that is, except Renee and her small team of scientists.

"Hello?" Neo called out, hoping that she would hear Cole or Brian reply. Her voice echoed through the once bustling lobby. No one answered her greeting. She walked over to the security station that once housed six armed security guards in the building. They were all gone. She began to make her way to the stairs leading up to the third floor and the secure storage area where the paper kept all of the expensive electronic equipment it loaned out to its reporters.

The winding, spiral staircase led her up to the third floor as the metallic echoes of her feet resonated throughout the empty building. She began to feel uncomfortable, and she felt sweat roll down her back. Paranoia came with the territory for the reporters that she had known.

From time to time, Neo had received threats over the years from the people that she wrote about in her articles. She understood that the least amount of suspicion was actually a good thing. With everything she had witnessed and experienced over the past few days, a large order of suspicion was necessary to help keep her safe and alive.

The top of the stairs led out to the second-floor lobby and a small waiting area. A row of cushioned seats, where visitors could look out through the windows to the street below, lined one wall. An office-lined hallway led away from the lobby. It was where the suite of editor offices were located, and also where the main meeting room, and the publisher's office was found.

The security locker was in the editor in chief's office, the last office on the left, almost at the end of the hallway. For the entire time that Neo worked at the *Times,* she had only been upstairs to this floor twice. One time during her initial job interview, and the second time for a staff meeting. It wasn't a place a staff reporter ever felt comfortable visiting. If a journalist found themselves on that floor, it normally meant they had been summoned by the editors, which usually meant that they likely screwed something up big time.

Neo made her way down the hallway and found the door of the room she needed to get into near the end. A gorgeous, brass plaque fixed to the door had text embossed on it that read *Pamela Mayfield.* Below the name was, *Editor in Chief.*

Pamela was, or had been, a great edit and boss. She kept out of the way of her reporters for the most part, giving them enough freedom to feel like they weren't chained to their desks. She was always willing to roll up her sleeves and get down in the trenches with her staff if she was ever needed.

Pamela had begun her journalism career writing obituaries at the *Times* nearly forty-years before Neo was hired, breaking the then male-dominated glass ceiling on her way to the top. Neo thought very highly of her.

Pamela managed to keep her femininity intact while still commanding the respect of both her male and female staff. That hadn't made her a pushover by anyone's standard. She was still more than capable of being a *bitch* if the situation warranted it. Tough, but fair, Neo would surely miss her.

Neo pushed down on the door handle and stepped into Pamela's office. A huge mahogany desk occupied the center of the room, and four matching mahogany bookcases, each filled with old milestone copies of the *Times* and reference books, sat off to one side.

One the wall behind the desk, Pamela had framed and hung many of the awards she had won during her long, illustrious career. A small room that set back slightly to the left was where Pamela had kept kept the security cupboard, and where Neo hoped to find the satellite phones Renee asked her to grab.

The cupboard was a big, metal storage cabinet with a large padlock looped through the handles. Neo gave the padlock a wiggle to make sure it was still locked. It was. She then felt around the top of the cabinet for a key, but found nothing except dust on her fingertips and on the palm of her hand. She frantically wiped the dust of on the side of her jeans. Neo had her fill of *dust* the past couple of days and didn't want anything else to do with any of it, in any form.

There was no key pinned to the wall or anywhere else in the room that she could see. She walked back into the main office area and began searching Pamela's desk drawers. When that turned up nothing, she turned her attention to her desktop, shuffling files and papers around hoping a key would be under the paperwork on her desk. Nothing. She was going to have to resort to a more basic solution.

She shook her head as she thought back to her experience with the fire hatchet. It would have come in handy right now. Her butcher's knife was too small for this job. The cabinet's hinges were located behind the doors, safely out of reach of any pry bar or screwdriver. Neo's only option was to find something big and heavy and try to break the lock off.

The janitor's closet was located on the main floor, where the cleaning crew kept their brushes, mops, ladders, and other equipment. The chance of finding something capable of opening the cupboard doors would hopefully be found in there.

Neo left Pamela's office and jogged back along the hallway to the stairs. She trotted back down to the main news-desk area. As she opened the door into the newsroom, an acidic odor punched her right in the face. It was a familiar smell...ammonia. She stopped with one hand still holding the door open.

"Damn, that shit stinks."

One of the monster things was in the immediate area, or had just left. The urge to turn and run out was overpowering, but the smell of cat-urine was nowhere near as lethal as she had confronted in the baby's closed up apartment, but it was definitely in the air, biting at her nostrils like month-old moldy laundry.

Neo searched throughout the expanse of the newsroom. Everything was exactly as she had remembered it. It actually looked as if her colleagues had just gone home after a long day at the office. Rows of L-shaped desks, neatly lined up like London soldiers in a parade, still held notes and paperwork.

There were a few laptops exactly where he owners had left them. The large TV screens on which she had watched the breaking newscast from Europe with her co-workers now showed only gray and black static dots.

***

Neo walked to the other side of the newsroom. Her sneakers squeaked against the vinyl-covered floor. The wall on her side of the room was clear of obstructions, except for a large photocopier, along with a collating table next to it. If she kept her back to the wall, she would have a good view of each row of cubicles, which would offer her a sense of safety and protection.

Neo paused for a moment to pull the butcher's knife out of her backpack as she inched her way along the hallway with one hand flat against the cool wall surface, the other holding the knife at a – *Go ahead. Make my day.* – ready-position. With each careful step, she scanned the dark recesses and shadows of the cubicles, watching for any movement. She had seen enough horror movies in her life to know that the threat always came when the character least expected it. She wasn't going to fall for that one.

As she walked past the middle of the newsroom, the vague outline of something across the far side of the room caught her attention. It was impossible to tell what it was, but she was familiar enough about the interior layout of the room to know that whatever it was in there wasn't there when she left the office the day of the ooze rain.

While in the doorway just minutes ago, Neo obviously didn't see the creature. It attached itself just out of her view to one of the large silver air-conditioning ducts that ran along the room's ceiling and down the opposite wall. She stood motionless, her eyes fixed on the odd shape, waiting to see if would move. It was tough to get a clear view of what it was because of the deep shadows surrounding it. If she had been focusing entirely on the cubicles, she likely would have walked right past it.

She took a cautious step forward. There were no signs of movement from the creature on the wall, but she kept her arm, with the butcher's knife in hand, extended out in front of her just in case as she pointed the steel tip of the blade directly at the creature.. If it jumped off the wall at her she was going to bludgeon it. That was the plan at least.

With each step closer to the creature, she was able to make out a little more detail of it. It was about four-feet long and two-feet wide. The head, if that's what you want to call it, was shaped like a large bullet. Its body body tapered off to a flat, gooey base at the opposite end. Its wet-like skin glistened a yellow-red, filled with bright red veins that intertwined over the entire length of its body.

As Neo took another careful step closer, she watched its veins intermittently pulsate as juices pumped through the length of the veins. Inside its see-through skin, she could see the shadow of a darker shape inside it flex and rotate.

As Neo gathered the courage to take yet another step closer to it, she stumbled on something lying on the floor. She was so focused on the creature thing on the wall that she hadn't paid attention to where she was walking. She went flying to the floor.

She instinctively dropped the knife while reaching out to grab hold of the nearest desk to brace herself from the fall. She wasn't able to stop herself from hitting the floor, which caused her to let out a loud *"oomph,"* which knocked the wind out of her. Somewhat dazed, she was able to get herself back to a standing position.

"Damn it!"

She picked the butcher's knife she had dropped and redirected her focus back to the creature on the wall. She glanced down and stared at what caused her to trip. It was a second creature. This one resembled a larger, menacing, fattened up caterpillar.

"Now that's fucking creepy."

Being so close to the creature, Neo could actually feel warmth oozing from it, yet nothing like the dense warmth of heat the baby monster in the upstairs apartment had given off. This was more like the warmth generated by a naked human body. She could clearly see thick, gooey fluid as it pumped through the arteries just below the surface of its skin.

She also could see a thinner integrated network of veins, like spider webs, spread across its whole body. Underneath its body, another shape moved slowly while rotating in red fluid, filling the interior cavity behind the creature's husky outer layer.

Before even Neo realized what she was doing, she reached out and touched its skin. It was slimy and warm to the touch. The dark shadow inside its body gave a sudden twitch when she touched it. Startled, she she yanked her hand back.

She was now aware that she had just touched something that had once been human. It now seemed in the process of becoming something entirely different. What that something was, she had no idea. She assumed that it had once been a co-worker at the *Times,* maybe someone she knew and was close to. Her mind shifted back to the day the ooze rain came and a conversation her and her colleagues held in this very room.

"Oh, God, no," she said out loud. "Please, no."

Was that Pamela inside the creature's body? Cole? Brian?

"Jesus," Neo said shaking her head as she studied what likely was the final remains of one of her co-workers. The ooze rain had come from nowhere. It killed everyone she knew and loved. If that hadn't been enough, it was now changing them into something else, something *alien,* with no resemblance to the person she had once known.

Neo looked around the floor for her knife that she had dropped when she tripped on the alien creature. She soon found it just under a nearby cubicle, and grabbed. She inspected the blade to make sure it wasn't damaged. It was still intact and as sharp as ever.

Neo walked out of the cubicle and stepped over the alien creature on the floor. She stood directly over it, placing a foot on either side of it and stared down at it. She was captivated, yet afraid of it. She then took a deep breath, and with the knife in her right hand, she raised her arm high above her head and plunged the knife down hard into the alien creature's body.

There was a gooey "pop" as the blunt tip of the blade punctured the body. Immediately after, a barf-inducing odor of ammonia slapped the shit out of Neo with a spray in the face of thick, yellow-red ooze that exploded from the alien creature.

Some of it also splattered on her T-shirt, jeans, and her exposed arms. She quickly made sure her mouth was closed so she wouldn't swallow any of it, but some did land on her lips. She backed away, reached around and pulled the back of her T-shirt to the front of her face, and wiped the stench of ooze off of her mouth and face.

On a nearby cubicle sat a container of hand sanitizers. She ran over and grabbed the whole container, then spent she spent several minutes cleaning herself off as best she could. She didn't have a change of so she had to wipe her T-shirt and jeans off as best she could, while at the same time keeping an eye on the creature on the floor, as well as its alien friend on the wall.

Neo then cleaned the knife off, walked back over to the alien on the floor, and stabbed it several more times for good measure, driving the blade even deeper in its body. The moving object inside its body convulsed after the stab-bings, jerking and writhing violently.

Putrid yellow-red fluid oozed out from the gashes in its body. The strong ammonia odor soon became nearly un-bearable as the moving entity inside the alien creature's body gyrated in pain. Neo knew what she had to do to finish the thing off. She stabbed it again several more times until there were no signs of life within it whatsoever.

Neo snapped her head around and turned her attention back to the other alien creature still clinging to the wall that she had seen earlier. She needed a ladder to get to it as it had migrated higher up the wall and out of her reach. Perhaps it knew it was coming next.

With her knife in hand, she scampered out of the news-room and down three flights of stairs back to the janitor's closet on the main floor of the newspaper. There, she found an medium-sized aluminum ladder. She carefully put the knife into her back jean pocket at an angle so as to not stab herself in the back as she tilted the ladder forward at her side, then jogged back up the flight of stairs to the main newsroom.

When she got there she stopped short of the entryway and gently walked in, using the ladder as a barrier between herself and whatever else might be lurking in the room. Careful to not trip this time, she methodically took the same route as before to where she had killed the alien creature. When she got to the exact spot, much to her horror, the damn thing was gone. She was *sure* she killed it. Guess not.

Neo lowered the ladder parallel to the floor and began searching for any clues as to where the alien had slithered off to. A quick glance at the wall confirmed that the second alien creature had now inched even further up the wall and closer to one of the air-conditioning duct vents in an attempt to either shield itself, or hide and pounce on Neo if she came near that wall.

She knew she had to get to the other alien on the wall before it snaked its way through the vent and out of sight. Because these aliens were super-slimy, she didn't doubt that they could easily ooze their way through the slits of the vent and disappear.

A triple-check of the floor, under nearby desks, tables, around corners, on the walls, essentially confirmed that the alien she just killed, or thought she killed, was nowhere to be found. She ran back over to where she had placed the ladder, grabbed it, and walked with purpose to the wall where the other alien creature was attempting to make a slow getaway. She knew she had to hurry because the alien, even though it was moving at a snail's pace, was getting closer to the air-conditioning vent.

She propped the ladder against the wall, made sure it was level and balanced, then climbed onto the first rung. She paused to purposely bounce herself around and lean to the left and the right to ensure she wouldn't fall once she got near one of the top rungs of the ladder.

Neo had surprisingly long arms. She made it to the second rung from the top of the ladder and reached up the wall with the knife in her right hand while pressing her left hand against the wall to brace herself. Leaning to the right and reaching higher still, she gritted her teeth and swiped the tip of the blade from side to side at the alien still clinging to the wall.

"Shit!" With each unsuccessful swipe of the blade, she could hear a *swoosh* sound. She was about six inches short of slicing that thing up. Determined, frustrated, and now pissed off, she carefully climbed back down the ladder, but stopped at the third rung from the bottom and surveyed the floor to make sure the other alien that got away didn't come back for revenge. The floor was clear. Neo hopped down and scanned the room, trying to find something long, like a stick or a broom that she could use to knock the alien off its perch on the wall.

Adjacent to the newsroom was a small recreation room where overworked, underpaid journalists could utilize for relaxation and entertainment when they were stressed with deadlines to meet or during slow news days. There was a pool table in the corner of the room.

She bolted to the recreation room and snatched a pool stick off the wall near the pool table. She turned and sprinted out of the room before caution got the best of her, forcing her to again scan the floor for any signs of aliens.

Convinced that there were none, at least none that she could see on the floor, she grabbed a female co-worker's sweater off the back of the woman's cubicle chair, then ran back to the ladder, the knife in her right hand, the pool stick in her left hand.

When she got to the ladder, she paused and cut two holes in the sweater where she estimated her eyes would be, and slipped it over her head to avoid anymore ooze slime squirting in her face again. She placed the handle of the knife in her back pocket again, and pulled herself back up to the second rung from the top of the ladder.

With the reach disadvantage problem solved, she used the tip of the pool stick to prod the alien, poking and jabbing around its gooey, jiggly underbelly, trying to dislodge it from the wall.

"C'mon down you little bastard. Yeah, that's right. After I knock your ass to the floor – I'm *fucking* you up."

The poking and jabbing caused stinking ammonia to ooze from the alien and down the side of the wall. Neo was fortunate this time as the creature was to the right of her and not directly over her, saving her from ooze dripping onto her.

Several more jabs and, "I got you!" she shouted. Neo heard a *slurp* sound as the slimy alien peeled from the wall and fell to the floor. She tossed the pool stick aside and backtracked back down the ladder. The impact of the alien slamming to the floor must have knocked it loopy as it lay on the floor twitching and oozing.

Neo didn't waste time exchanging pleasantries with it as she pulled the knife from her back pocket and began to stab and slice the alien's body with rapid thrusts of her knife. She wasn't about to wait around to watch what might be inside this one.

As she sliced up the alien, like the other one, it sprayed yellow-red ooze all over the walls and again onto her clothes and at her face. This time, she was better prepared for the odiferous trajectory of ooze. Satisfied that it was dead, at least incapacitated for now, she hurried out of the newsroom and didn't look back.

***

Neo knew she had to make it back to the security cabinet. If she didn't break into it soon, grab the satellite phones, and get the hell out of the building, she would have major problems getting far away from Los Angeles. With the knowledge that the alien creatures can apparently defy death, she had no idea how many more of them were out there.

She used up the remaining sanitizer wipes and dabbed at the ooze that had splattered on her arms and hands. After she finished cleaning up, she headed back downstairs to the janitor's closet. There, Neo struck gold yet again in the Janitor's closet. She found a sledge hammer, and charged back up the two flights of stairs to where the security cabinet was located.

When she arrived at the cabinet, she studied the padlock securing it to estimate how many strikes it might take to break it off. She figured three or four would do it. With four two-handed powerful strikes at the padlock, it gave way and broke apart into two pieces.

With the lock issue solved, she dropped the sledge hammer and pulled the metal cabinet doors apart. Inside, she found what was was looking for on the top shelf. There were two satellite phones housed in a canvas carryall about the size of a woman's handbag, with the word "Iridium" stenciled on the sides in large yellow letters.

Neo pulled the bag from the top shelf, sat it on the floor, unzipped it, and snatched out the contents, laying them next to the bag. There was a satellite phone, charger, operating instructions, an extra battery, and a solar charger in its own water-resistant case. The other satellite phone the *Times* had was missing. Perhaps someone else grabbed the other one on the way out during the ooze rain catastrophe.

She quickly tossed the items back into the bag and searched the cabinet again for anything else that might be of use. There was nothing left but a locked cash box that likely contained a few thousand dollars. She paused, nodded her head, and decided to take that with her, too.

She likely wouldn't need any cash, as it seemed that any bank, store, or business in Los Angeles was now her personal cash box. As she closed the door to the cabinet, she picked up the sledge hammer and carried it with her along with the phone equipment, and zipped the bag closed.

Neo retraced her steps back along the hallway and down the metal staircase. She could still feel the adrenaline rush pumping through her body from killing the two alien creatures. She then realized there wasn't enough time tonight to do any shopping for additional supplies at Wal-Mart as it was fast approaching dawn.

Her plan was to drive back safely to her apartment, hunker down for the night, pray that that there wouldn't be another alien creature encounter, get a good night's rest, then load up the Mercedes with everything she had, go shopping at Wal-Mart, and begin the day-long drive to Grand Forks, North Dakota to meet up with Renee and her team.

Neo made it safely out of the *Times* building. Dark shadows were visible on the street as the sun had set behind them. A row of streetlights had already begun to brighten the street.

Before she began her drive home, and remembering what Renee had said about being extra careful to search the interior of with whatever car she found, she realized she hadn't yet checked the trunk. What if a dead body was in there, or one or two of the alien creatures? She walked around to the back of the car, pushed a button on the electronic keypad, and popped the trunk open.

Whoever owned the beautiful car was meticulous. There were very few items in the trunk, except the obvious spare tire and hand jack, a bottle of windshield wiper fluid, a couple of cans of engine oil, and a container of radiator fluid, all neatly arranged. Satisfied that there was no danger, she closed the trunk, walked back to the still open front car door, took another quick glance behind the seats, hopped in, started the engine, and sped off in a pronounced hurry.

During the short drive home, she relived the events of the day and felt proud of herself in the choices she had made. However, she knew she couldn't continue to battle those creatures, as she was surely outnumbered. Time was of the essence. Those things were continually morphing into God only knew what. Neo didn't want to stick around LA any longer than one more night to see what the creature's final transformation might be. That would be a real-life horror story that she didn't want to see come to fruition.

***

As she slowly rounded the final corner before arriving at her apartment, she scanned the areas in front and at the sides of the building. She opened the car door, slid the car keys into her jean pocket, took hold of her sledge hammer, grabbed her backpack and stepped out of the Mercedes to fling over her shoulder, then reached back inside and picked up the bag carrying the satellite phone equipment. She felt like she just went grocery shopping, and had arms and hands full with plastic grocery bags.

With her free hand, she pulled the knife out of her backpack. Armed with a knife and a sledge hammer, she was confident that she could hold her own if an alien creature tried to attack her. Neo delicately walked toward the front door, then stopped to exhale and relax a bit from carrying such a heavy load.

Her relaxation moment was short lived. Who knew what might be waiting for her inside her building since she had been gone for the past two hours. Several dreadful scenarios raced through Neo's mind. What if one of the alien creatures somehow made it into her apartment while she was gone?

What if the baby alien creature had mutated into an adult stage, and was waiting for her for round two of their earlier brief introduction? What if a horde of the ugly, slimy, slithering bastards were waiting for her just beyond the front door of the building, and surrounded her as she walked in?

Thankfully, a portion of the entry door contained clear glass. When she got to the door, she leaned her face flush against it and peered inside the lobby area. Her eyes zipped up, down, left, and right. Seeing nothing, she slid the knife under her armpit and punched the electronic eight-digit security code number to open the right side of the double doors.

Successful, she then raised the head of the sledge hammer, pulled the knife from her armpit and extended the blade of it, and nervously swung the door open using two fingers while holding the knife. She braced the door against her ass on the back swing, and stepped inside.

Neo wasn't about to become a detective and begin searching for any creatures that might be lurking around, so she walked as quickly as possible toward the path of least resistance – the stairwell. She pulled the stairwell door open and poked her head inside. It was all clear, so she stepped inside and bounced up the stairs to her seventh floor apartment, her backpack slapping against the notches of her spine. She stopping periodically to catch her breath as her hands and arms began to burn from carrying so much equipment.

Stopping at the stairwell door leading into the hallway on her floor, she paused. The stairwell doors contained a small, square window that Neo used this time to visually inspect the hallway for any ooze filled aliens on the floor or stuck to the walls. Again, she saw nothing and pushed the door open with her foot and stepped inside the hallway.

She was excited to see her apartment down the hallway about fifty feet away. She gripped the knife and sledge hammer even tighter, readjusted her backpack around her shoulder, took a deep breath, and sprinted as fast as she could to her front door.

At the door of her apartment, she shifted the knife into the hand holding the sledge hammer and fingered her car keys out of her pocket. She had previously transferred her apartment keys over to the Mercedes key chain for convenience. She was glad that she did, because it only took seconds for her to unlock the door.

With extreme caution yet again, Neo poked her head just inside her apartment. By this time the sun had set completely and it was dark outside. It was also dark inside her apartment, too, as she had not even thought about leaving any lights on before leaving for the *Times* earlier. Her head was still tucked inside her apartment while her body was still standing in the hallway. With a free arm, she quickly found the light switch. When the side table lamp blinked on, it caused her to catch her breath and brace herself for the unexpected.

At first glance at the floor and walls, and much to her relief, her apartment appeared to be in the same condition as when she had left it. She hurried and locked the front door. She still needed to do her due diligence and check each and every room from top to bottom to be sure an alien creature wasn't hiding in wait. She thoroughly searched the living room, kitchen, bathroom and behind the shower curtain, closets, her bedroom, and lastly, under the bed – *nothing.*

Safe for now, she understood that she was going to risk draining the water she had collected out of the tub and running another hot bath. She was going to soak in it for as long as necessary, then try and get a good night of unmitigated sleep before heading out again at sunrise.

After running her bath and stepping inside the tub, Neo submerged her shoulders into the hot water until the soothing waves caressed the underside of her chin. She exhaled, then closed her eyes. She was looking forward to enjoying soaking her exhausted body for an hour or so.

Suddenly, all of the lights went out.

OOZE

14

NEO WAS THE KIND of woman who never feared the dark.

When she was a young girl, and none of her friends could sleep without having a small desk lamp on, she had laughed. She was never one to believe in the whole *monster hiding under the bed or in the closest concept.*

In fact, she never hesitated when exploring the fields of her parent's farm after dark, curious as to which animals were making certain noises in the woods at night. Oftentimes, she would find a patch of grass and sit to watch the sunset and gaze at the moon and stars.

This was a different type of darkness. It was profound and absolute. She might as well have been blind as she tried to step out of the tub in sheer darkness without slipping, falling, and breaking her neck. She reach over and grabbed the towel she had hung on a small chair next to the tub.

After drying herself off, she slipped on a pair of fresh jeans and another T-shirt, and maneuvered her way, her arms extended out in front of her, and her fingers as hand guides, through the black abyss of her apartment.

She knew that there was an emergency generator in the basement of the building that should have automatically activated and turned on the backup lights when the power shut down. For some unknown reason, that didn't happen. She correctly decided that it would be much too time consuming, not to mention, risky, to try and search each room for it. Instead, she chose to rely on her natural senses to guide her to the basement.

No lights meant no floor numbers, either. When she walked out into the hallway, then the stairwell, she had to count each level as she went, and hope she didn't miscount and end up on the wrong floor. She began counting each flight of steps out loud. It wasn't long before the sound of her voice echoing down the empty shaft of the stairwell irritated her and made her more uncomfortable than the eerie sound of her footsteps.

When she made it safely to the basement, she felt around for where she thought the door should be. It wasn't there, so she moved her hands over a few inches and found the crack where the door met the frame. Her hands then found the coolness of the pane of security glass in the door's center panel and she slid her hand down from there until she felt the aluminum bar-handle.

She was set to pull the door open when a barely audible noise caught her attention back at the stairwell. It was distant, but for sure coming from within the building somewhere. It was a creepy gurgling sound that bounced off the walls. It wasn't like anything she had heard before the past few days.

She heard the sound again. It sounded like an animal digging and scratching for something, or someone. As Neo listened, there were a few more strange sounds that joined the initial one, answering the call as if two animals were having a conversation in their own language. She wasn't too concerned until a third noise in the stairwell was without question, much closer to her. *Forget about turning the emergency generator on now,* she thought. That so was *not* happening.

***

Neo flung the door open and staggered blindly out into the total darkness of the hallway, and shoulder-first into the opposite wall, jarring her body. The repulsive cry of the unseen alien creature again echoed up from the stairwell, causing her to go into a mini-panic attack...yet again. She was completely disoriented because the hallway was just as pitch black as was the stairwell. She had no clue whether she was facing forward or away from her apartment upstairs.

Run like hell! She thought to herself. Where? Which way? She smacked herself upside the head. *Ow!* She admonished herself for not keeping a flashlight in her apartment ready to use for exactly this type of situation.

She didn't want to just take off in any direction and end up in the wrong half of the hallway, or worse yet, fall down and seriously injure herself, only to become a wounded, easy target for the aliens. She decided to remain exactly where she was. Her heart pounded and her breathing intensified.

There was no mistaking the fact that she was indeed afraid of *this* dark.

Neo could hear other noises such as shuffling and sliding sounds that filled the empty air. It seemed to come from every floor of the apartment building. Was she now surrounded by aliens? Did the alien creatures somehow compromise the electrical system to cause all of the lights to go out? She figured there must now be an entire army of them, fully mutated, and ready to seek revenge.

She *was* surrounded. She reached into her jeans and pulled her apartment keys, her saving grace, from her pocket. Even though she couldn't see her keys, the reassuring clank of metal against metal was a cherished sound of normalcy and, if she could just recount her steps again and find her front door up three flights of stairs in total darkness, that would be awesome right about now.

She took in another deep breath and reached out with both hands. Her hands connected with the wall of the stairwell as she felt her way along the wall's surface, and began walking up the stairs. She counted the levels as she went, and soon made back to the seventh floor. She now instinctively knew which direction to head to arrive at her front door, but she would still have to rely on her sense of touch to make it the rest of the way.

Neo heard something cry out from the other side of the stairwell door that she had just walked away from and into the hallway. In the darkened hallway, her remaining senses switched into another gear. She knew that one of the creatures she had earlier heard in the stairwell was now *a lot* closer to her.

Suddenly, a deranged, ear-splitting scream bellowed from the alien in the stairwell. The scream was forceful and menacing, causing the walls and floor beneath her feet to noticeably shake. Neo gasped, turned, and ran in the direction of her apartment, clutching her keys. She extended her right hand to feel each separate door of the apartments, counting them one-by-one, until she came to her apartment, which was the fourth door on the right.

She ran as fast as she could to the last few steps to her front door. Her hand made contact with her door just as she heard a click and the familiar squeak of the stairwell door slowly opening. She stopped, turned her head toward the stairwell door, and braced herself..

The hinges continued to squeak. Behind that sound was another noise she had not heard before. Her eyes grew larger and she was so afraid that she literally stopped breathing for several seconds. The slippery, slurping sound of something large as it squeezed itself through the doorway echoed down the hallway. It was followed by another noise, like tap dancing shoes on a hardwood floor, the sharp "tap, tap, tap" of multiple feet clicking against the floor was like an alien who had just made its grand entrance into the hallway and began moving in her direction.

Tap...tap...tap...the rhythmic, repetitive sound crept closer to Neo, then stopped for a moment before continuing.

She began to quickly feel around her door for the lock. Finally, she felt the cold metal of the knob beneath her trembling hand. The keys on her key chain slipped between her fingers several times as her hands were soaked with sweat.

Tap...tap...

The sound was even closer than before. Now, she could smell the alien. Her breath blew out in short, began to come out in short, jagged bursts of pure fear and panic. As the alien in the hallway was getting increasingly closer to her, it must have sensed her fear, much like a crazed, rabid dog senses fear in its target before viciously attacking it.

Neo let out a huge scream. "Get the fuck away from me!" causing the alien to suddenly accelerate toward her more quickly. Even if she hadn't forgot to carry her butcher's knife and sledge hammer with her, they likely wouldn't have done much good because she could hear the alien, but she couldn't see the damn thing.

Tap...tap, tap, tap...

Neo fingered the keys to find the correct door lock by feel, while at the same time groping the outline of the brass lock cylinder against her fingertips. She matched them up perfectly, slid the key inside the lock, turned it, and let out a quick sigh of relief at the sound of the all too familiar click of the lock opening.

She twisted the knob, pulled the key from the lock, and the weight of her body pushed the door open, causing her to make a flying entrance into her apartment. She turned and slammed the door closed, locked it securely into place, and fastened the security chain.

Neo thought to herself that it's definitely true about what the popular song says: *"The Freaks Come Out at Night..."*

Standing in complete darkness in her apartment, she took a glance out of a window. The streetlights were out also. She knelt down on her hand and knees and crawled along the short hallway until she came to her bedroom. She rushed inside, still on her hands and keens, over to her small walk-in closet on the near side of the room.

Opening the door to the closet, she crawled inside, barricaded herself in with the clutter of clothes, shoe boxes, and a tiny filing cabinet, and anything else she could find, intent on remaining in there until the sun came up in the morning.

She got herself comfortable, closed the closet door...and waited.

15

The Fifth Day

NEO COULDN'T RECALL what time the alien creatures stopped their dreadful cries. As the night wor on, her mind offered her the only protection that it could, providing her with a cushion against the overwhelming sense of *I'm going to die* that gripped her as she listened to the creatures crying out to one another all night long.

Her body simply shut down at some point during the night, allowing her to fall asleep. When she awoke, the memories of the previous evening came flooding back to her, and they brought with them a new worry, that while she slept, the aliens that she had heard in the hallway outside of her door, had somehow gotten into her apartment.

She had no clue how long she had taken comfort inside the closet, nor did she know what time it was. It didn't really matter. She was still alive. Soon, her dark closet revealed a bright light of hope that filtered through the crack in the middle of the door, only to mean that daylight had finally come.

As she shook her head to clear the fog of sleepiness, she grunted in pain as she eased her body away from the wall she had fallen asleep against. When she tried to stand, using her right arm to push herself from the wall, both of her knees made a "cracking" sound, and her calves cramped up as she unfolded them beneath her, causing another round of grunts.

She wobbled to a full standing position as she stood silent in the darkness, and waiting for the blood throughout her body to recirculate again. Her thoughts turned to her next challenge – whether or not aliens were outside the closet door, or outside her front door waiting for her.

Neo reached for the closet doorknob and, ever so carefully, twisted it, cringing as the latch squeaked. Keeping her hand firmly on the handle, she pushed the door open until a crack large enough for her to view her bedroom and the door leading into it was visible. She was ready to slam the closet door shut again if she saw anything creepy.

There wasn't any sign of a disturbance, so she pushed the door open a few more inches until the gap was wide enough for her to stick her head through. She scanned the rest of the room and the back of the door, just to be sure nothing was hiding out of sight.

She peered out through the crack in the middle of the sliding closet doors and saw nothing that warranted a screaming fit. She opened the closet doors, while at the same time feeling vulnerable to the world, and walked out of her closet fortress and into the bedroom.

She stepped over to the bedroom door and glanced out into her hallway, and again, nothing. The front door seemed to still be in one piece. The thumb lock and security chain were also both still in place. Relieved, she knew she would still have to investigate her entire apartment before she could completely relax and look forward to her long drive to Grand Forks, North Dakota.

She opened her bedroom door and began searching the rest of her apartment. Moving from room to room quickly, it was clear to her that whatever had been lurking about last night had lost interest in her and never ventured inside her apartment. Her humble abode looked exactly as she had left it; nothing waited for her in any of the closets or behind the breakfast nook, or even under her bed. Sweet.

Neo walked back to her bedroom to unpack the satellite phone and accessories. She carefully inspected them for any damage and all seemed well and good operating condition. Then she pressed the power button on the phone. The display went blank. The battery was dead. She flipped the plastic backing off, pulled out the old battery, and inserted the spare battery, in hopes there would still be some charge left in it. No go. It too was dead. Great. She needed to charge both batteries in a hot minute.

She glanced over at her bedside alarm clock. The alarm's display was blank. She walked over to the light switch on the wall, flicked it on and off a few times but the light above her head did not turn on. With the power still obviously out, and with scant chance of it ever coming back, she was going to have to use the solar charging unit she had grabbed with the satellite phone to charge the batteries.

It was vital that she reestablish a line of communication with Renee and her team in North Dakota as quickly as possible as they needed to be informed of what was happening.

She opened the box containing the solar charger and read through the instructions on how to operate it. The device came equipped with a separate battery unit that plugged into the collapsible solar panel. This separate unit would hold a charge for up to eight times longer than a regular battery, and would allow her to then charge the phone's batteries from the unit.

This meant that she would always have an extra charge at her disposal. The only problem was, it would take around six hours to fully charge the solar unit *and* then the phone. Not good news.

She was itching to get *out* of Los Angeles, not continue to stick around and offer herself as an unwilling target for the aliens out there roaming around somewhere.

Neo took the battery unit and solar panel to the living room where it would absorb the most sun. On the way in she checked the clock on the cooker, realizing she had no idea what time it was, so she had to go by the battery-powered analog clock on the wall that read: 12:10 P.M.

That meant she would have at least nine hours of sunlight to take advantage of. It should be enough natural energy to get a full charge. Unfortunately, having to wait for the batteries to charge would delay her in getting out of Los Angeles and away from those ever frightening aliens, but she had no other choice.

Yet again...she waited.

With the easy to follow details in the instruction book to guide her, she made quick work of assembling the unit. She snapped each piece into place, then moved the completed unit to the sideboard close to the window where the solar charging panel could gather all the energy it needed.

Instantly, a small red LED indicator on the top of the unit began flashing to show that it was indeed charging.

Neo's stomach growled loudly in disapproval of being ignored. She had to put her hunger pangs on the back-burner for right now while she worked to get the unit up and charging. With that chore out of the way, she figured she had time to feed her belly.

When she opened the refrigerator a wave of cool air escaped from the interior. She knew that wouldn't last too much longer now that the power was shut off. She had half of a Wendy's hamburger sandwich left, along with a six-piece box of chicken nuggets. She decided it was best to eat them both before spoiling. She downed the meal with the last half-full glass of sweetened ice-tea, then took a couple of aspirin from the medicine cabinet in the bathroom to stifle a small headache.

With her stomach full, Neo turned her thoughts to the next item on the day's to do list: getting out of Los Angeles.

She had recalled that the gas gauge on the abandoned Mercedes that she selected off the street still had half-a-tank, so she didn't need to gas up anytime soon. Besides, she can stop by any gas station along the way after going shopping for more supplies at Super Wal-Mart.

She made a short-list of what she might need: an emergency medical kit, tons of bottled water, and a gun or a semi-automatic rifle with plenty of ammo, to name a few. The butcher's knife and sledge hammer served her well up to this point and was definitely coming along for the trip, but she also wanted something with more *"I'll blow your damn head off"* firepower.

She was confident that when she eventually leaves Los Angeles, if she chooses the right routes, she can avoid the major population centers. If she stuck to the rural areas, she could find a safe place to sleep in her car for the night while hopefully reducing the chances of meeting up with more aliens. If she could manage that, then she wouldn't have to worry about carrying more than a day or two of food and water supplies with her. That meant less stops along the way, except for refueling.

***

Neo made her way into the bathroom of her apartment. What she saw looking back at her in the mirror startled her. She raised a tentative hand to her cheek and touched her pale, gritty skin and gently probed around the puffy dark circles under her eyes with her fingers. It had obviously been a long, grueling several days which seemed to age her beyond her twenty-five years.

She noticed that her hair was a tangled mess, with flaky pieces of dust and dirt sprinkled around her head. She would have loved to run another hot bath, soak for an hour, and wash her hair, but that wasn't possible for now. There was no time for common luxuries, or for any extended attention to physical hygiene at this point in time.

She would have to simply settle for washing her face and body with a hand towel, and washing her hair in the sink. If the regular water supply system to her apartment was shut off soon, she could always just wash her hair using bottled water. She hoped to take a nice, long hot shower when she got to Renee's headquarters in North Dakota.

Neo slipped out of her dusty T-shirt and jeans, changed her underwear, balled them all together, jumped up in the air, and tossed them into the corner of the bathroom as if she was shooting a basketball into a hoop. Without electricity for doing laundry, she wasn't going to be wearing them again anyway, nor was she concerned about coming back to the apartment later to clean the place up.

She allowed the reality of that thought to sink in. There would be *no* coming back. Between the ghost towns of Los Angeles and Grand Forks, she hadn't given it much thought about whether Grand Forks will even be intact when she gets there.

From this point on, it's...here to nowhere.

***

Before leaving for the drive to gather supplies and gear, Neo wanted to make sure she would be better prepared for another unwelcome encounter with an alien along the way. She gathered together the sledge hammer, her butcher's knife, several bottles of water, and a bag of miniature Snickers candy bars that she found in the stockroom at the candy store. She packed everything except the sledge hammer into her backpack and tossed it over her shoulder on the way to the front door.

With one eye, Neo squinted through the peep-hole for any sign of aliens in the hallway. It looked clear. To err on the side of caution, she raised the head of the sledge hammer in a ready position before slowly opening the door. Turns out, there was absolutely nothing outside her apartment waiting to kill her. The hallway was quiet and empty.

However, there *was* something different.

Several shredded holes underlined the wall on the far side of her apartment. They were extended along the back toward the door to the stairwell before bending up onto the ceiling and ending at the stairwell entrance. Neo leaned in to get a closer look at the holes. She noticed that they were large enough for her to put her thumb in and seemed to have been sliced up by something sharp enough that it left a clean hole void of any rough edges. They looked like track marks.

A mutated alien creature had indeed come up through the stairwell last night. While Neo had struggled in the darkness, it climbed along the hallway wall in pursuit of her and stopped outside her apartment. The thought of it sent mega chills through her body, causing a hard shudder in reaction.

Her eyes danced instinctively up and down the hallway, along the walls, and the ceiling as she triple-checked to be sure that the alien creatures weren't hiding somewhere nearby. She guessed that the creature was rather large, at least three or four feet wide, based on the the track marks on the floor. They must have also been responsible for the power outage. The two circumstances that occurred last night at around the same time seemed just too premeditated to not somehow be related.

Her only hope of avoiding round two of last night and surviving was to continue with her plan, which entailed leaving Los Angeles. She had people waiting for her – *real human beings*.

***

Neo's walk down the stairwell was much easier and less stressful than the previous night. She followed the tracks she found outside her door as they continued along the wall of the seventh floor and eventually into the darkness of the stairwell.

The lobby of the apartment building seemed clear. Nothing looked out of the order, but she did notice more than three other sets of tracks leading from the ground floor, and out through the building's main doors. That meant there were a horde of aliens on the loose. The good news was, the tracks appeared to be heading out of the building and away from her.

Neo was happy and excited to be able to step onto the sidewalk outside her apartment building and enjoy the fresh air and sunshine. Now that she was fully committed to leaving, her apartment had gradually become more and more claustrophobic than comfortable. It now served as an old, abandoned, inhabitable relic of the past, and no longer home.

The Los Angeles sun was sparkling and bright, with not a cloud in the sky. It reminded her of the weather on the same day the ooze rain fell. The sights and sounds that were once the heartbeat of this great city seemed so distant. She took some comfort in knowing that she wasn't the only survivor, and this would be the last day that she would have to spend in this vast city of ghosts and aliens.

Holding the keys to the Mercedes, she walked up to it and again inspected the interior and exterior for any evidence of alien invasion – nothing. She hoped in, fired up the engine, took a deep breath and a final glance around the area of her apartment building she used to call home, and sped off in the direction of Super Wal-Mart.

As she drove slowly through the eerily empty streets, past stores, businesses and deserted sidewalks, she took time to take it all in, remembering what her city used to look like. As she made a right onto Vermont Avenue, Neo had to suddenly swerve in order to miss hitting a large snack food delivery truck jutting out from the nearly collapsed building front it had collided with. The street was littered with snack food items such as Twinkies, Ho-Ho's, Nutty Bars, Oatmeal Crème Pies, and the like. Apparently a snack free-for-all took place here not long ago.

The goodies lay scattered across the streets, mixed in with the debris from the ripped apart building. The cab of the snack truck had buried itself deep inside the obliterated building. Splintered floorboards, pieces of ceiling, and plasterboard hung from the entrance of the building.

Neo got out of her Mercedes and began to make her way through the debris and wreckage, careful to avoid sharp splinters of wood and exposed nails jutting out like daggers from every angle. When she got to the truck, her reporter's curiosity got the best of her.

Both doors were closed, but the passenger side window had a nearly perfect circular hole in it measuring a few feet across, similar to the dimensions she noticed in the hallway outside of her apartment. She took advantage of the truck's footplate to step up and investigate the hole. It seemed as if an alien creature had taken a circular saw and cut through the glass, or whatever had made it had chewed through the glass.

She ran her fingers over the sharp edge of the opening. Peering through the hole into the cab, she could see that nothing remained of the driver. The person had disappeared. In their place was the remains of one of the large caterpillar type alien creatures she had seen at the *Times* yesterday.

Both doors of the truck were still locked from the inside, meaning that one of the aliens had killed the driver, and made its exit through the circular hole in the glass. The hole was simply too perfect to have been caused by the crash. Neo's logical guess was that it could only have been caused when the alien found itself trapped inside the cab.

She turned her attention back to the remains of the caterpillar-like alien excess lying on the floor of the cab. It had split open along its midsection like a huge clam shell. The inside was a dark brownish color, but she could make out several gooey looking tubes that she thought had acted like umbilical cords to feed the alien creature the nutrients that it needed. A faint, familiar stink of ammonia still filled the truck's cabin.

Neo climbed down from the truck when suddenly, a laser beam of fear enclosed itself around her. The realization that this was going to be a long day had cemented itself in her mind and body.

***

Based on the information Renee had given her earlier, Neo knew that in order to get to North Dakota in a timely manner, she would be crossing parts of Nevada, Utah, Wyoming, and South Dakota. The thought of the trip overwhelmed her, so she planned to break the drive up into smaller four-hour intervals, in hopes of making it more manageable.

She decided she would drive for four-hours straight, then rest, eat, and find shelter to sleep, unless she would find it safe to sleep in the Mercedes. Seeing as how easily the alien creature clawed or gnawed its way through the glass window of the snack truck, caused her to have second thoughts about catching a few winks in the car.

A lone police car, its lights still flashing atop the roof and its front driver's side passenger seat windows rolled all the way down, blocked the left lane of the road near Super Wal-Mart. The cruiser was positioned to stop any traffic from continuing beyond it. As Neo slowly drove toward abandoned police cruiser, she pulled alongside the driver's side, stopped, got out of her Mercedes, and leaned in, her eyes quickly searching its interior. She located exactly what she was looking for sitting between the passenger and driver's seat.

She reached down and pulled out a shotgun.

"Hell, yeah!" she shouted in victory as she held and studied the powerful Benelli M4 tactical 12 gauge shotgun. She also found plenty of spare shells in a box under the seat. After a bit more digging in the interior and in checking the trunk, she also found a sling, two bandoliers, a shotgun belt, and a shell holder.

"Saddle up, Neo," she told herself.

Neo knew what each of the items were, except the bandolier, which she had never heard of before. The only way to know what it is was to use her common sense. A bandolier is a military style shoulder belt with loops or pockets that carry cartridges. The one she was holding came with loops. If she so desired, she could strap both loops over each shoulder and across the front of her chest and back for quick access to ammunition and easy transportation of her weapon.

"So that's what a bandolier is," she confirmed to herself.

The previous summer, Nick had insisted on teaching her how to shoot, and had taken her to a gun range. While she had enjoyed learning the ins and outs of firing a handgun, she had mostly enjoyed shooting a shotgun.

Neo liked the heft of it, but she really enjoyed that whatever she pointed it at was likely going to be destroyed. It could effectively hit a target as far as one-hundred yards away. At close range, the shotgun was absolutely lethal. The Glock 9mm pistol Nick had handed her was just her size, and had left small holes in the paper target she was firing at, but the shotgun shredded the paper.

While she wasn't sure just how effective the shotgun might be against alien creatures, she definitely felt safer in knowing she now had something more effective and powerful to defend herself with.

***

As Neo made a left turn onto West Cesar E. Chavez Avenue, where the new Super Wal-Mart is located, there were four cars that had collided at the intersection. Two were yellow taxicabs, one was a white Honda Accord, and the last one was blue Chevy Blazer.

One of the taxis had broadsided the Honda, and the second taxi had apparently slammed into the back of the first taxi, blocking the intersection. Two police cars, one on each side of the street, had positioned themselves to stop or direct traffic flow.

She guessed that the accident must have occurred during the ooze rain. She was shocked to see that the lanes that were blocked by each patrol car, had rows upon rows of empty cars, trucks, buses, and motorcycles. Obviously caught up in the infamous Los Angeles traffic congestion, each driver had likely been sitting impatiently in their vehicles unaware that the hot, grimy street would serve as their tombstone and final resting place.

The exit lanes leading away from the traffic lights were more or less empty, apart from the occasional vehicle caught in the process of making a U-turn, hoping to head in the opposite direction of the accident before it was too late. Neo noticed that one truck had run through a bus stop, scattering bits of destroyed shelter across the sidewalk and street.

There was no sign of an ambulance, thus the accident likely happened moments before death stepped in Los Angeles.

Neo made a wide turn around the debris of the accident. She got out of her car and began to search the vehicles for any signs of life. Their engines must have all been running at the same time the ooze rain fell because, inside every vehicle she looked into, the keys were *still* in the ignition. Many had their doors closed and locked.

Several unlucky drivers had apparently managed to get their doors open before succumbing to the effects of the ooze rain. Every locked vehicle she walked by had one thing in common: they had an almost perfectly round hole in one of their windows as she had seen earlier in the snack delivery truck.

She made her way back to the Mercedes amazed by what she had just seen. Whatever type of alien creatures did this made quick work of the drivers and their passengers of the stranded vehicles. Neo drove up to the front of Super Wal-Mart, strapped the shotgun and ammunition to her chest, locked her car, and walked toward the electronic sliding front doors.

Before she made it to the front door, it occurred to her that the parking lot was completely empty of customer and employee vehicles. She could only assume that they had all hightailed it out of there once the ooze rain began to do its damage. Many of those same people were likely a part of the rows of cars stranded in traffic nearby.

Much to her surprise, the front doors to Super Wal-Mart were locked. She leaned her face against the tinted glass to look inside and noticed that everything seemed normal. She walked back to the car and pulled out the sledge hammer, then walked around the bumper to the rear of the car, popped the trunk open, and grabbed the tire changer crowbar.

She trotted back to the front doors and wedged the flat end of the crowbar in between the slit of the electronic doors. She then shifted her weight to the right, extended her arms, and pulled on the crowbar handle as hard as she could – nothing. She tried once more and again, but had no success in opening the doors.

She realized she would have to get in the hard way. She picked up the sledge hammer, widened her stance to shoulder length, and with both hands gripping it, she turned her head away from the door before she reared back, lifted a leg, and followed through with force. It was like a hitter in baseball timing his swing before striking the ball with the bat, sending the head of the sledge hammer crashing into the glass of one of the doors.

The glass shattered into a thousand tiny ice-cube like shards. She took a quick step back to avoid the avalanche of glass before it hit the ground outside and landed just inside the doorway. Once the initial damage had been done, Neo used the bulky head of the hammer to knock out the remaining small loose panes of glass. She pounded away at the glass and carved herself out a large enough hole that she could bend down and walk right into in the store.

As she took a moment to admire her handiwork, she began to lower her head and slipped inside. If the power had still been on, the alarm system would have sounded off. Instead, only the crunching sound of broken glass under her sneakers accompanied her into the next level of the store. Carrying her sledge hammer with her, once inside the front doors she was happy to see that the second level of electronic doors leading in the main floor were already open.

The interior of the store gradually became darker the farther back she ventured from the sunlit entryway, but there was enough light coming through the vast amount of windows on the walls to see things clearly.

Neo grabbed a nearby grocery cart, her mind was focused on quickly gathering supplies and getting the hell out of there. First and foremost however, she was concerned about her own personal safety. She had no clue if one of those aliens creatures was somewhere inside the store slithering around.

She made certain to search the floors and poke her head cautiously around corners, and in between clothes racks where one of the creatures could be hiding. After a thorough search turned up nothing, she backtracked to the center of the store. She walked quickly back along each of the walls of different departments and snatched up everything she thought she might need for the drive to North Dakota.

After bypassing the stench of rotting meat and vegetables, she tossed into her cart bottled water, several cans of Chunky soup and other non-perishable canned foods, a few large boxes of brand name cereal, several of graham crackers, a heavy-duty sleeping bag, a Mercedes-Benz compatible car battery from the automotive department, numerous bags of Snickers candy bars, a red large-sized plastic gasoline container, an eight-cell Bright Star flashlight and batteries, eating utensils, a GPS unit to help with directions to North Dakota, two pair of new jeans and matching tops, underwear, a pair of new sneakers, hiking boots, two heavy jackets, socks, and a few boxes of feminine hygiene products.

After she collected everything she could think of, she pushed the grocery cart full of items to the front of the store. When she passed the level of doors leading to the main entrance, she realized the hole in the glass that she had made wasn't large enough to push the cart through.

She tossed the items that were in her cart through the hole, two and three at a time, before crouching down one last time to step and leave the store. She then walked back to her Mercedes, checked the interior for aliens, and seeing that there weren't any, hopped in and backed the car up to the entrance sidewalk, and popped the trunk open. After tossing her stash into the trunk, she was ready to hit the highways.

As she drove out of the Super Wal-Mart parking lot, she again approached the near mile-long traffic jam of empty vehicles. Rather than take the same route she had arrived to the store, Neo decided to cut through known side streets to make her getaway onto the freeway, but not before stopping at a local gas station to fill up.

Once the tank was full, she planted her foot down on the pedal and sped across town on her way toward I-15 North freeway and North Dakota.

OOZE

16

BY THE TIME NEO realized it, she was three hours into her drive and already in the state of Nevada. The time had flown by, at least for now. Her mind had gone through an extensive replay of the past week that was, including every detail that she saw, heard, and felt.

She blinked and shook her head back to consciousness. She was thankful that driving was much like riding a bicycle; once you learn the basics, your mind is pretty much on automatic, allowing her to essentially drive without thinking about the actual act of driving. It wouldn't have mattered anyway as she was the only human being on a freeway filled with abandoned vehicles.

Prior to the ooze rain, she remembered Los Angeles as it used to be: people busy leading their lives on various social and economic levels. Lives that were suddenly and horrifically ended. People had been transformed into alien creatures. What is the purpose of these creatures, and why are they here?

She hoped to find the answers to those questions and more from Renee and her team. The potential answers were still hundreds of miles away. Neo became exhausted from the trance-like state from driving for three hours straight and needed to sleep.

A solid line of gray clouds tinted by an aura of red had begun to descend as the sun began to set. The wonderful Nevada weather could not have lasted much longer. Neo found herself missing the implied sense of security that the past few days of clear blue skies had offered her.

She doubted the thick cloud would bring any rain, or ooze rain, for that matter, but it would bring a sense of heaviness to the air that would cast a lethargic net over everything. She hoped the change in weather and natural scenery was not an omen of the darker days or darker things to come.

Neo couldn't keep her eyes open any longer. Even though the Mercedes she was driving was the one and only mechanical moving object on the road, she didn't want to fall asleep at the wheel and die from injuries caused by crashing into the rear of an abandoned semi-truck. She wasn't going to go out that way. She decided to pull as far off the side of the open freeway as she could, hoping that once darkness fell, her car wouldn't be easily noticeable.

She drove about a mile more when she spotted a string of abandoned vehicles in close proximity to one another, also facing north. There were at least fifteen vehicles along this stretch of highway. Some had been parked in the middle of the road, while others were pulled over to the side. Neo decided the best way to remain safe was to blend in and pretend that her vehicle had also become abandoned, thus hoping to avoid looking different than all of the vehicles she had passed along the way the past three hours.

As the dark clouds crept closer, she found what she thought would be a safe place to spend the night in her Mercedes. She pulled the car in between a big rig, and a large, four-wheel drive SUV with huge off-road type tires and rims.

There, she figured it provided a cushion from being seen by possible oncoming traffic or traffic from the opposite direction, yet also giving her a clear view of the expanse of barren land surrounding her. She also believed the location between the two vehicles would allow her to make a quick getaway if alien creatures happened to stumble upon her in the middle of the night while she slept.

The Nevada air was similar in temperature to Los Angeles, but Neo knew that the farther north she drove, the colder and wetter it was going to get, forcing her to later change from lighter clothing and into cold weather attire.

With barely any daylight remaining, and feeling confident about where she had chosen to spend the night, Neo was happy that the Mercedes was equipped with dark tinted windows, further offering her a sense of protection. It allowed her to see outside, without anyone, or anything, seeing inside the car easily.

Her stomach reminded her that she hadn't eaten for a while, but she was more exhausted than hungry. She did a last minute inventory and check of her shotgun, ammo, butcher's knife and sledge hammer before soon quieting roller-coaster like thoughts circling in her head. Finally... she drifted off to sleep.

The Sixth Day

Neo awoke to a new day painted with beaming rays of Nevada sunshine. She checked her fully charged satellite phone and noticed that it was nearly 7:30 A.M. Starving, she sat up straight in the car and surveyed the landscape for anything out of the ordinary.

Everything up this point had certainly been out of the ordinary, but she still wanted to make sure one of those creatures wasn't waiting to attack her outside her car door.

She reached over, pulled a spoon from the console, and opened a can of Chucky Beef soup while allowing her mind to drift toward her plans for the morning. A top priority was to get to Grand Forks, North Dakota, of course. She had been taking the most direct route there so far.

Her train of thought was jolted by the sound of something scratching underneath the Mercedes. Her spoon of soup stopped halfway to her mouth. Her head cocked to the right as she listened to see if the noise would reappear. Sure enough, there it was again. It sounded like something skittering across the ground while their body rubbed up against the underbelly of the car. Was it trying to escape, or was it trying to get to her? Neo didn't know the answer, but she was sure about to find out in a hurry.

She thought it would be much safer to stay inside her locked vehicle rather than exit and investigate the noises. As she listened, she heard an eerie, high-pitched howl rising up through her car from directly beneath her car seat.

Within moments, something scratched at the bottom of the car again, as if a mechanic was loosening the filter for an oil change. The continued groan was similar to a call of desperation. So too was the baby, who had earlier seemed to cry out for help above her apartment, only to wind up being a disfigured alien creature.

All thoughts of food vanished as Neo dropped her spoon into the can of soup and sat the container on the front passenger seat. The noises continued, as if something was trying to dig its way through the metal under the car. She placed her hand on the middle of the steering wheel and blew the horn three times.

The scratching and clawing noises stopped as suddenly as they began. A few moments of silence followed, interrupted only by the occasional sound of something still moving underneath the car. Then she heard a loud thump as something heavy hit one of the muffler pipes. She popped her head up and glanced at her rear-view mirror, then each of her side mirrors, but saw nothing.

She thought about simply starting the car and driving away, dragging whatever was under there with her. However, what if that didn't kill it, and the next time she stopped somewhere the same scratching noises that's happening now, happens again later?

Neo decided to get bold. After all, she had a shotgun handy, and liked her chances of killing whatever was trying to kill her under her car. She reached down at her feet, grabbed the shotgun, unlocked and slowly opened the car door while pointing the barrel down, ready to pull the trigger.

She caught the movement of something dirty and hairy that had just scampered back under the car. Was that a cat? She gasped and leaned her head back into the car, slammed the door shut and locked it again. She then heard another strange, but familiar sound...wailing. The kind of sounds that an animal would make if it were injured and desperate for help.

She wasn't going to fall for that one again.

She could hear it scratching again and again at the metal underneath as though trying to cut its way through. It sounded to Neo as if it was somehow trapped. Perhaps it had gotten itself tangled up underneath the car somehow overnight. It didn't sound happy to be there.

Still clutching the shotgun tightly in her right hand, she unlocked and opened the car door again. This time, knowing that the thing was still underneath the car, she jumped out and ran about twenty feet away from the car, all the time holding the barrel of the shotgun at ready position. Then, she waited – nothing.

She leaned down as far as she could to take a good look underneath the Mercedes but couldn't see anything or even the shadow of anything dirty and hairy. Still leaning down, she placed the shotgun on the ground next to her and got down on all fours to get a better view of it. Suddenly, whatever was underneath her car sprang out from a blind spot on the other side of a tire and ran like a cannon-blast directly toward her.

"Shit," she hissed through clenched teeth as she scrambled back to her feet, reached down, grabbed the shotgun, took a deep breath, and pointed the barrel at the thing racing toward her. She braced herself for the thundering jolt of her weapon's kickback at any second and began to squeeze the trigger, then she *froze*.

"Well, I'll be damned," she said to herself, lowering the barrel of her shotgun.

The furry, dirty animal with its tongue hanging out from the side of its mouth, its ears straight up in the air, and its wet nose glimmering from the sunlight, happily bounced toward her before stopping about ten feet away.

It stood in place panting with its tail whipping from side to side, studying Neo, who in turn studied it. It was an awkward encounter. She immediately could tell that it wasn't an alien creature because its excited demeanor wasn't anything she had gotten from the aliens.

She further lowered her shotgun to the side of her leg, knelt down on one knee, and placed the shotgun on the ground beside her.

"Come her, boy," she said softly. "I won't hurt you, I promise."

The animal barked twice at her without moving an inch. "It's okay. I'm one of the good guys," she said with a broad smile.

The animal, sensing that she offered no physical threat, hung its head and began to walk slowly toward her.

"Come over here and let me take a good look at you, you mangy thing."

The animal continued walking cautiously toward her before stopping five feet in front of her. Neo slowly reached out her hand as a friendly gesture. The animal came a bit closer, sniffed her hand, and took a step backward.

"I don't have all day you know. Either come here and meet me up close or I'm leaving, and you'll be stuck out here to fend for yourself."

She and the animal made close, direct eye contact for the first time. The stare down lasted several seconds. The animal took another step closer. She again reached her hand out in friendship. The animal sniffed it again, and this time gave her hand a few friendly licks. Neo leaned forward and patted its head as it slowly inched to her.

"How long have you been out here little dude?" she said, scratching under its furry chin."

The animal, now easily recognized by her as a normal American dog, crawled up into her chest and began licking under her chin.

"You smell rank, buddy, you know that?" she said chuckling and fanning her nose with her hand. "But I've smelled much worse than you the past few days," she said. "I'm still gonna need some serious hand wipes after this."

She was elated to finally have something friendly and non-threatening to engage with. She would have preferred another human being, but a dog is the next best thing, she concluded.

"What's your name? Let me see if you have a collar on with your name on it under all that hair."

The dog had a collar, a blue one, but it didn't have an aluminum name tag attached to it, but she saw that it was a male dog and that it looked relative healthy despite its coat being dusty and dirty.

Arf! Arf!

The little dog leaped from her lap and ran off about ten feet before stopping, turning, and barking again.

Arf! Arf!...Arf! Arf!

"What is it, boy?"

The dog ran back up to Neo as she stood up. It nudged its nose against her leg a couple of times before running off, stopping, turning, and barking at her again.

Arf! Arf!

"Sorry, I don't speak doggy language. Are you trying to tell or show me something?"

The dog growled at her this time, as if it was becoming annoyed that she didn't understand what it was trying to tell her. Instead of trotting back to her, it took off running toward one of the big rigs abandoned on the highway.

Neo scooped up her shotgun and followed several tentative feet behind it to the big rig. When the dog stopped at the tractor-trailer, it barked even more insistently. She now knew it was trying to alert her to something or someone inside the truck's sleeping cabin.

She had now become experienced at this kind of thing as she raised the barrel of her shotgun chest high, expecting the worst, and prepared to defend herself if need be.

Arf! Arf!

"Okay, boy. I'm right here. Let's see what you've got there."

***

Located in the sleeping compartment of the tractor trailer truck was the mutated mass of the dog's two owners. They were still alive and moving. The little Terrier started barking at them as if to introduce them to his new friend, Neo. The now double-headed creature began to shake as if attempting to rise up from a horizontal position. It looks as if it had pulled in its legs and curled itself snugly in a ball.

The creature suddenly flicked out its four oozing, bloody legs at once as they snapped into place like the sound of a plastic click. The alien creature rose to a sitting position and shook itself like a dog after an unwanted bath, sending gooey bits of ooze and blood splattering against the interior walls of the sleeping cabin.

Neo had never previously seen one of the creatures grow to advanced stages...until now.

Its four eyeballs extended and the eyes popped open, staring directly at Neo. With the shotgun still in her hand, she slowly backed away. The dog started to bark fervently and spun around in circles as if it was playtime.

The creature's jaws quivered with a warning growl, and it slithered out of the sleeping cabin and took a couple of off-balance slow steps toward her with all four legs measuring different heights. Neo in turn reached down and scooped up the little dog with her free hand as she continued to retreat backward.

Thoughts rushed through her mind. *Should I get in the car and drive away, or should I just blow its two heads off and ask the dog questions later?*

She continued to take small steps backward as the dog continued to bark hysterically while tucked in her left arm as she continued to point the shotgun at the creature with her right hand. She kept her eyes focused on the alien while trying not to make any sudden moves causing it to become aggressive.

As she ever so slowly back peddled, her ass rammed into driver side door of the Mercedes, stopping her momentum. She had to make a decision, and quickly. The creature had kept pace with each of her steps backward, even on four disfigured legs. The stare down began, and for a moment, time stood still.

It stared at her for a few seconds from ten feet away. Neo never blinked.

The creature then leaped into the air and sprang toward her. This time, she wasn't taken by surprise as she sidestepped the alien creature, dropping the dog. It then turned around and came back at her again with viciousness, stopping within three feet of the dog she had dropped.

Neo feared for the dog, thinking the alien was going to kill it and then her. She could feel hot blood surging through her cheeks as her face became distorted in anger. Before this day, she would have succumbed to unimaginable fear.

But this was a new Neo that this alien creature was dealing with.

She knew what she had to do next.

The dog, now frightened and realizing the alien was no longer its loving owners, shivered in silence with its head lowered, ears flat against the back of his head, and his tail tucked tightly between his legs. The alien creature gave another, louder growl as it scanned Neo as if to assess her threat potential.

The creature reached out its enormous left limb, that which now combined two dead people, and leaned down toward the frightened little dog. Neo moved her right hand quickly to the cylinder of the shotgun and placed her finger on the trigger. She had no idea what the alien's intentions were, but if it thought she was going to stand by and let it kill an innocent, defenseless dog, well...*Not. Gonna. Happen.*

Neo raised the shotgun to her chin, securing the butt of it against her shoulder, and fired away.

Boom! Boom! Boom! Boom!

She blasted the creature with two shots to its double-sized head and two shots directly into its torso, sending chunks of bloody, gooey mass everywhere, causing the creature to jerk violently backward and fall to the ground. Neo edged toward it ever so carefully as she watched it convulse and leak slime-like blood from its head and body as result of the massive wounds from her shotgun.

She fought the urge to grab the little dog and sprint to the car.

She scooped the dog again and walked about twenty feet away from the creature before turning back around to see if it had moved. There was no movement in it whatsoever, not even a final gasp of life. One of its four eyes was still intact from the previous blast, dangling off to the side an unrecognizable face.

She had seen these things die, only to quickly come back to life again and vanish. To be as certain as she could be, Neo stooped down to place the dog on the ground, walked back over to the hideous looking alien creature, and calmly shot out its remaining bulging eye, blasting it into gooey pieces.

Something brushed against Neo's leg and scared the crap out of her. It was the dog. She had been so focused on the seemingly dead alien, waiting for it to spring back to life, that she momentarily forgot about the little pooch.

She looked into the dog's eyes and smiled. It then cautiously walked toward its former owners and sniffed at the still oozing, dead carcass before turning up its nose after getting a whiff of its putrid smelling ammonia, and galloped back behind Neo's protective legs.

"Sorry, Charlie," she said looking down at the quivering dog, then turning to gaze at the dead alien again. Neo cocked her head to the side and chuckled at what she had just said. That's when she knew exactly what to name her new companion – *Charlie*.

After thoroughly cleaning Charlie with water and drying him off with one of the towels she had confiscated from Super Wal-Mart, the two new friends were ready to continue their journey. Neo was in a great mood after killing the alien creature, who never moved another inch long after she had killed it.

The two friends hopped in the Mercedes, Neo turned on the radio and listened to music as she sped off. She wanted and needed to put aliens out of her mind for awhile, especially during the long drive from Nevada to Utah.

Twenty minutes into the drive, she channel surfed several other radio stations and stopped when she heard an old, famous song that her parents used to enjoy singing to during road trips while they all giggled and laughed.

Playing on the radio was Willie Nelson's *On the Road Again.* In honor of her dead parents, with tears streaming down her face at the memories of them singing the song to her when she was a young girl, Neo now found it fitting to sing it to Charlie.

"On the road again. Just can't wait to get on the road again. Going places that I've never been. Seeing things that I may never see again. I can't wait to get on the road again..."

Neo turned to Charlie and laughed. "Yeah, no shit, huh Charlie?"

OOZE

17

NEO PULLED THE MERCEDES over to the side of the road just inside the Utah state line. Charlie needed to either take a piss, drop a deuce, or both.

She opened the car door and he hopped out in a hurry, scampering to a large, nearby tree. He sniffed around the tree, turned around four times, and lifted his leg close to the tree's trunk. Neo had gotten out of the car to stretch her legs. She leaned against the front end of the car as she watched her new friend do his business.

She took the break from driving as an opportunity to reload the shotgun, just in case, then put it back inside the car, laying it across the back seat.

The sound of something big moving around up in the tree caused Charlie to cut his pee break short. Neo gazed up into the tree and froze in place. Whatever was up there didn't seem to be in a particularly friendly mood. She uncrossed her arms against her chest and tried not to make any sudden movements.

She then slowly leaned over, opened the car door, and reached inside for the shotgun on the back seat. She pulled it out of the car and shoved the butt of the shotgun against her right shoulder to reduce the impact. She raised the barrel and aimed it at the middle of the tree as she stood about twenty feet away.

The branches and leaves gyrated again, this time catching Charlies' attention. The little mutt naturally began to bark at the sounds and movement, jumping up and down on his short legs as if he was going to get up into that tree and kick some ass. Yeah, right.

"Charlie, no!" Neo yelled out. "Get over here, now!"

Charlie continued his barking frenzy, circling the tree and jumping up against the trunk of it in an attempt to get to whatever was up there. She knew he wouldn't listen to her so she began to walk toward the dog and the tree with her shotgun pointing directly at the rustling branches and leaves.

She sucked in a huge lungful of air and concentrated on calming her nerves as she waited for whatever was in the tree to make the first move. Neo tried to focus on relaxing her hands; they gripped the shotgun so tightly her knuckles had turned white. She spread her feet wide and with the front sight of the shotgun drew a bead on the spot where she thought the sound was coming from.

The crackle of movement and the sway of branches on the left side of the tree grabbed her attention. Whatever was moving around was no bird or squirrel. This was something much larger. Charlie let out one last vigorous bark before he suddenly changed his attitude and demeanor with an ear-piercing squeal before sprinting to the comfort of his new owner. He took refuge behind her legs while continuing to bark his little head off.

The thing that sent Charlie running for his life jumped from the tree to the ground. It was another melted mass of mangled flesh and body parts – an alien creature. This one was much larger than the others had been. It more resembled an actual adult human figure. It began to limp slowly toward Neo, its three eyes stalking her like a predator eyeballing its prey.

Neo took two steps backward, nearly tripping and falling over a frightened Charlie, who was clinging to her ankles. She swung the shotgun around and pointed it in the direction of the alien monster. Sweat popped on her forehead, trickling down into her eyes, and it burned.

She pushed the stock of the shotgun tightly back into her shoulder. She released the pistol grip and used her free hand to wipe the sweat from watering eyes as the alien creature continued to limp toward her while dragging one of its other deformed legs across the ground, stirring up a cloud of dust. Her hand moved back to the shotguns' grip when a huge shape exploded from the inside of a nearby abandoned vehicle twenty-five feet away.

She turned and staggered backwards in surprise, accidentally stepping on Charlie's back right paw, hearing him shriek in response. "Sorry about that, buddy." After steadying herself, Neo looked up and saw the creature was a mere ten feet away from her and Charlie. The two made instant eye contact.

It bore little resemblance to the alien-caterpillar creature or the midget-alien creature from the big rig that she had already encountered. This alien creature looked more like a regular animal with a human body. It was about six feet long standing and hunched over, and walked on three muscular, mutilated legs.

Its body was covered in long spines that stretched backward from the tip of its neck. They were muscular and powerful looking. The spines were colored varying shades of red and light brown that gave the alien creature a striped camouflage, allowing it to blend in with the natural foliage. That's why she nor Charlie detected it earlier.

Instead of a normal head, there was a mass of articulated yellow-red tentacles as long as an arm. Each slender tentacle moved independently, and stretched out toward her, writhing and twisting like a pit of snake heads. It seemed as though it was assessing the air for her body temperature or her smell. Perhaps it was attempting to determine how much her blood pressure increased, caused by a level of fear.

In the middle of its torso were three eyes along with the flailing tentacles. A long muzzle of a mouth opened wide to reveal row upon row of jagged teeth. The alien's head bobbed back and forth excitedly as it tracked her movement while she scrambled backward. The alien opened its mouth wide and Neo could see its yellow tongue flicking back and forth between the rows of teeth.

The creature moved in closer Neo, its head dipping low then back up again like a man shoveling snow with each each step it took. She wasn't as nearly fearful of the alien creature in the big rig, but this one was bigger, stronger, and more menacing than the others. For a split second, she even wondered if her shotgun was adequate enough to stop this particular alien, or at least slow it down long enough for her and Charlie to get to the car.

However, her feet refused to move. She was tired of running away. Now, she's pissed off. She grunted, swung the barrel of the shotgun up and pointed it directly at the alien creature standing ten feet away from her and a still barking Charlie.

The creature must have sensed her newly discovered aggression as the spines covering its body vibrated loudly, giving off a threatening rattle, and launched at her, jaws wide open, tentacles striking as it accelerated toward her.

Neo gritted her teeth, aimed at its heart, and pulled the trigger.

She heard two *booms* of the shot and felt the butt of the shotgun slam violently back into her shoulder. The alien growled and squealed in pain as it slumped to the ground with a heavy thud.

It was still alive. The blast from the shotgun had caught it just above where she had estimated the heart to be. Perhaps she was wrong, and its heart was located elsewhere within its body, which wouldn't be a surprise to her. The second blow created a gaping hole in its abdomen. It oozed yellow fluid. Writhing in pain but still very much alive, its right leg hung loosely at its side twitching, while the remaining two legs flinched uncontrollably as the creature tried desperately to right itself and stand.

Neo wasn't having any of that. She easily could have shredded the thing with more blasts from her shotgun, but this thing wanted to kill her. She wanted to send it a message loud and clear, and to any other aliens out there who might be hiding in the landscape somewhere and watching: Neopolitina Kao was no longer afraid.

She ran back to the Mercedes while still carrying the shotgun as Charlie kept pace at her ankles., She opened the door and reached into the back, grabbing the sledge hammer laying across the floor below the back seat.

Now it's payback time in a truly personal manner. Neo wanted to bash its fucking head in, then watch it continue to suffer until it died for good. She knew that if she didn't force herself to finish this beastly looking alien off, it was still more than capable of killing her and Charlie, even in its badly injured condition.

"Stay, Charlie. I mean it," she said sternly, careful to keep herself and her dog new dog out of range of the alien's blade-like tentacles, sharp teeth, and its snapping jaws. She walked quickly up to the alien before stopping a foot or so from its body. She looked down and studied it, and saw that it still had shallow breathing, but no movements anywhere else on its sickening mass of a body.

Neo reared the sledge hammer back with both hands and swung hard at its head. The forceful impact caused its head and remaining eyes to explode into a gooey mush, like a watermelon. She stood tall over the motionless body of the dead alien, her chest heaving as she sucked in huge gulps of dry Utah air.

In contrast to the loud blasting and smashing, a silence encompassed the air around her and her dog. Charlie came trotting up next to her again, nudging his wet nose against her leg. She bent down and picked him up in her arms as they watched the alien exhale a final gurgling death howl.

"Charlie, you better be glad that I'm a dog lover, or that thing would have turned you into a tasty little snack."

Her new canine friend joyfully licked her chin in response, as if to thank her.

"Okay, okay. You're welcome. I've got your back."

"Arf, arf...arf, arf, arf!"

"You've got my back, too? Cool. I appreciate that, my dog. Now let's Willie Nelson our asses back on the road again."

18

NEO WAS THRILLED that there weren't any more alien sightings during the long, nighttime drive through Utah.

She had pulled over to the side of the road twice since killing the larger alien creature to let Charlie out to do his business again. It dawned on her that there was no reason at all to even pull over. Vehicles of all makes and models still littered the highways but she could have simply stopped in the middle of the road without any concerns about being rear-ended.

After Charlie emptied his bladder and hopped back in the car, she opened a can of Vienna sausages for him and watched him scarf them down. She pulled a small plastic bowl from under the passenger seat and filled it with fresh water for him. The smell from the can of food triggered a deep rumble in her stomach. It was lunch time for her, too.

Neo was actually in the mood for a tasty hot lunch in an internet café such as Starbucks. She knew that was no longer a realistic possibility, but it made her appreciate and miss the ambiance of sitting in a public restaurant, order-ing food, and enjoying it in peace and quiet. She suddenly realized she had taken it all for granted.

A can of Chunky New England Clam Chowder soup would have to do for a late lunch. She reached up, pulled down the sun visor, and let a silver spoon fall into her lap. She took time to appreciate and enjoy this quiet moment with Charlie. It was just the two of them this night; well, not exactly if you include the aliens, but she was looking for-ward to normal human interaction as soon as she arrived in North Dakota.

She finished her lunch and realized she too needed to go to the bathroom. Of course, being on a vacant highway void of other humans and nothing more than abandoned vehicles as landscape amid the darkness, led her to decide to simply squat in the middle of the road to relieve her bladder.

Finished, she checked the GPS unit of the Mercedes to determine how many more miles she had to drive to reach Wyoming. Much to her surprise, she only had 73 more miles to go. She was impressed with herself that she had made good time thus far, in spite of the alien encounters.

"Arf, arf!"

"I know, Charlie. It's time to Willie Nelson again."

Neo was a bit tired, but after the alien slithered out of the tree back in Utah, she couldn't risk being taken by complete surprise again by another of the those creatures. Those freaks would surely use darkness to their advantage in killing her and Charlie.

Onward she decided to drive, until the sun came up in the morning. She reached across her chest and shoul-der and strapped on her seat belt. She then looked over at

Charlie and smiled, rubbing the top of his head. The dog wagged his tail in excitement. Charlie trusted her, and in turn, she trusted him. They were a team.

"Charlie, why the hell am I putting this seatbelt on when there's nobody else on the road but us?"

"Arf, arf, arf!"

"Exactly! I don't know why I bothered, either."

***

The night seemed to last forever and Neo was becoming more tired, finding it difficult to keep her eyes open.

"Charlie, my man. I wish you could get behind the wheel and help me drive so I can get some sleep."

She knew she needed a quick wake-up call of some sort and got one in the form a large green sign just up ahead. Neo slowed down and flipped on the high beams so that her tired eyes could see it more clearly.

The sign read: *Welcome to Wyoming – Forever West.*

In the middle of the image was a man riding a bucking bronco and waving his cowboy hat in the air above his head in jubilation, against the backdrop of beautiful Wyoming mountains. Seeing the state sign gave her the instant boost of energy that she desperately needed. She glanced over to the passenger seat to check on Charlie and saw him curled up and sound asleep.

"Charlie, wake that hairy ass of yours up. We're in Wyoming, dude!"

The dog's head popped up quickly, along with his ears. He snapped his head from side to side from her to the side door window and back again. He lifted himself from his curled position and placed his two front paws on the dashboard to peer through the front window before realizing there was nothing to be excited in his mind, and proceeded to assume the same position he was just in.

Neo was able to drive through the rest of the night without falling asleep at the wheel. Good thing, as the sun began to ascend above the beautiful Wyoming mountainside. Thirty minutes later and just up the road on the right, she spotted a small diner. It was perfect timing she thought, because by now the previous day's lunch had made its way to her lower intestine. It was time to use the bathroom again. This time, squatting in the middle of the road wouldn't do.

She pulled into the diner, not expecting to see any humans, but certainly expecting to maybe run into an alien or two. However, the urge to use the bathroom overcame the fear of another alien confrontation. She was just going to take her chances and let fate dictate the rest of the day.

With her shotgun in hand and fully loaded, Neo studied a large square sign hanging above the diner entrance door that revealed its name: *Colby's Finer Diner.* How quaint, she thought.

She and Charlie got out of the car and walked up to the front door of the diner. Neo stepped to the side of the building to peer into the window to see if she could spot any trouble before they walked in. The diner was completely empty from her point of view, but there were areas inside that were hidden from the window. The only way to investigate it was to venture inside.

"Let's go in and take a look around, okay Charlie? Be careful, boy. If you notice anything weird, start barking."

"Arf! Arf!"

The two companions used extreme caution while walking through the front door of the diner. The strong smell of stale beer and cigarette smoke immediately greeted them.

It looked like any other typical diner along any stretch of highway in rural Utah.

As she walked around a corner wall with Charlie close by her side, something caught Neo's eye that frightened the living hell out of her. She stopped cold and jaw dropped as she gazed up at ten-feet-tall stuffed grizzly bear attached to a wide base stand. The grizzly bear was in full fur. Its lips were curled up exposing its sharp teeth, and an intimidating snarl was permanently etched across its face.

Neo reached out and touched one of its paw nails from two extended arms that seemed to be reaching out and and grabbing hold of her. She had never seen anything like it while living in Los Angeles, but remember seeing all types of stuffed animals while growing up on a farm, such as deer, bears, even lions and tigers. This bears' taxidermy was flawless, which maintained its real life aura.

"Hey, Charlie, is that a friend of yours?" she teased the dog. Charlie looked up at the stuffed grizzly, barked once, then ran back behind her legs. Neo had hoped that the bear on display was the only frightening thing she would come across inside the diner. Next up, she needed to find the bathroom, and did.

The diner contained the usual wooden tables and chairs, along with a bar where a patron could either order a beer, or pancakes, sausage patties, scrambled eggs and hot coffee. She could imagine the place hopping busy on a Friday or Saturday, the tiny diner packed with locals, waitresses or waiters buzzing around taking orders and delivering home-made meals amid friendly chatter and laughter.

Neo flushed the toilet and went to wash her hands, examining her face in the mirror. Her eyes were bloodshot with dark circles under them. Her hair was a mess again.

She desperately wanted to partake in the simple matter of hygiene and brush her teeth, but there was no time for that and she had left her toothbrush in the Mercedes. She rinsed her face with cold water, then wiped her hands with a paper towel and patted her face dry.

Her relaxed state of mind didn't last long as she exited the restroom.

Three alien creatures appeared within a few seconds of her walking out of the stall. She grabbed Charlie up into one arm while the shotgun dangled at her side in her other hand. She turned and ran toward the kitchen area to find a back door.

One of the alien creatures crashed through a long wooden table and chairs as they were closing in on her, the muscles in its legs bulging as they swiftly extended one gruesome looking leg in front of the other. Almost in unison, they leaped the last fifteen feet toward her, their tentacles flailing. As one, all three aliens let out startling cries, smashing everything within their path.

"Oh, shit!" Neo yelled out as she ran as fast as she could toward the back door of the diner, letting out bursts of breath as her legs kicked into gear. These aliens were much faster than any of the ones she previously encountered, leaving her no time whatsoever to stop and shoot at them.

She needed to create adequate distance between herself and all three of them in order to open fire on them. Her heart was pounding as she grunted through the kitchen and raced to the back door. The heavy pounding of the aliens' feet were getting closer. They were chasing her down like hungry hyenas after a helpless wildebeest.

As she came within ten feet from the back door and temporary freedom, she froze in her stride. *How the hell had one of them managed to get in front of me?*

This is bad. This is really bad, she thought.

Before in dealing with the aliens, Neo hadn't had to confront more than one mutated monster. Now, she has to somehow kill all three of these things in order to survive and live to see another day. She knew she was outnumbered, but she wasn't going to be outsmarted.

Now surrounded by all three aliens before she could exit out of the back door, she leaned down and gently dropped Charlie to the floor, who then went into a barking frenzy, which momentarily switched the creatures' attention away from her.

She then reached over with her left hand, picked up a small table leaning against a nearby wall, and flung it at the aliens. One of the creatures raised its tentacles and swatted the table away like an NBA in your face slam dunk rejection, smashing it to pieces. Gripping the shotgun with both hands, Neo raised the barrel chest high, aimed at the creatures, and pulled the trigger.

Click. Nothing happened.

"Fuck!" she screamed as the shotgun jammed. A shell must have gotten stuck in the barrel. Charlie preoccupied the aliens by circling them, growling and barking like a vicious dog three times his size. He was small dog, but quick, able to dodge the alien creature's sharp tentacles while playing keep away. Charlie was the perfect diversion that Neo desperately needed as it allowed her rack the slide to clear the chamber. She then raised it chest high once again, then called out to her brave little friend.

"Charlie! Here, boy – like right now, dammit!"

Charlie sprinted back to her and took refuge again behind her legs while continuing to bark. Neo pulled the trigger again fanning the shotgun from side-to-side, blasting all three aliens in the neck, head, and chest, as they advanced toward her. Another blast sent half of one of the alien's head spiraling into the air, trailed by a spray of yellow ooze, before slapping hard against a wall. Their tentacles flailed before one by one landing on the floor with a limp thud as their decapitated and annihilated bodies soon slumped over in heaps.

"Bitches."

Neo swept the barrel of the shotgun from side-to-side, up and down, searching for any signs of more alien creatures. She reloaded the shotgun with ammo in her chest holster as she wiped sweat away from her face. Air. Fresh air, to be exact. That's what she craved as the dead alien's bodies stunk like the all to familiar ammonia.

Neo leaned down, picked Charlie up once again before taking one last panoramic view of the kitchen area for any more signs of trouble, then turned and bolted toward the back door. She noticed something odd that caught her attention and stopped her in her tracks right before she got to the back door. She saw that the back door was ajar, as if something had either come in or went out during the shootings. She wanted to make sure there were no other aliens waiting for her on the other side of safety and freedom.

Neo brought the barrel of the shotgun chest high again. As before, she lowered Charlie to the floor. She stuck her foot out and wedged it between the gap and the door frame. Slowly, she inched the door wider with her foot, wincing as it squeaked from rusty hinges.

There was a slight rustle outside to the immediate right of the door. She stuck a portion of the barrel of the shotgun through the gap and followed it by poking a bit of her head close to the gap, allowing her to scan the immediate area outside with one eye. She didn't see anything nor hear anything strange. With a tentative step she lifted the barrel of the shotgun from left to right, ready to pull the trigger again at any moment.

Suddenly, a blur of motion in her peripheral vision quickly caught her attention. Instinctively, she pulled her head back inside, just in time to avoid losing it as a massive tentacle from another alien creature sliced through the air, barely missing her, and crashed into the opened door, splitting it in half. Neo felt her hair fly up as the tentacle swam through the air just past her face, sending her and Charlie flying backward and to the floor.

A fourth alien creature stepped into the kitchen and advanced toward her. Neo leaned to her left, pulled Charlie behind her back, lifted the shotgun to her waist, and fired away.

Boom! Boom! Boom!

All three blasts made direct contact to the aliens legs, torso, and head. Badly wounded, she didn't kill this one. Neo heard the alien cry out in pain and scramble out of the back door. She rose to her feet and ran to the door. She saw the alien galloping away with one less tentacle, a shattered leg, and its head split in two, barely clinging to its neck and shoulders.

"Oh no you don't, fucker!"

She took off running after the creature with Charlie sprinting right behind her. She knew she had to kill it for her own peace of mind and safety. As she came within twenty feet of the alien, she readied the shotgun, pointing the barrel at its head again.

Sensing Neo was quickly gaining on it, the creature stopped in mid-stride and turned toward her. Time stood still once more.

Neo and the creature were at a standoff. It was Déjà vu all over again. Her finger twitched on the trigger, waiting for the creature to make the first move and receive its fate. It just stared at her, its spine vibrating violently, and its mouth wide open in a vicious snarl.

Charlie stopped barking and again tucked himself behind Neo's legs.

What was left of the creature's muscles flexed. Its two remaining tentacles flicked about in an attempt to intimidate Neo. A few days ago, that would have definitely worked – *not today*. She smiled at the creature, glanced down at Charlie and winked at him, then fixed her stare back onto the creature, before finally pulling the trigger.

Boom! Boom! Boom!

The loud shotgun blasts echoed through the air and the Wyoming mountains as the shotgun shells tore through the alien's mouth and head, ripping through its remaining tentacles into a fine yellow mist of ooze, and exiting through the back of its skull.

A slew of alien brain matter went spinning into the air behind it. The creature flipped backward into a complete somersault and violently twitched on the ground. Its tongue hung from the corner of what was left of its mouth. Its legs gave a final spasm, a few kicks, and then it died.

Neo took a few steps closer to the alien creature to get a better look at the damage she had done to it. Charlie followed, his lips pulled back in a silent snarl as he eyeballed the creature and circled around its body, sniffing and snorting at it. Charlie then turned his back to the creature, and with his two hind legs, he instinctively scratched and kicked up dirt onto the creature's dead carcass.

Neo reached down, picked Charlie up in her arms and gave him a warm hug. In return, the dog licked her nose in excitement.

"Good boy, Charlie. You saved my life back there. If you hadn't kept those things preoccupied, we would both be dead right now. I'm proud of you, little buddy, and I love you. Now let's hop back in the car and get the hell out of Wyoming."

"Arf! Arf!"

OOZE

19

NEO LET OUT a resounding *"Woohoo!"* at the sight of the state sign welcoming her to South Dakota. The loud yell woke Charlie up out of a deep sleep. It was well into the night now.

"You know what, Charlie. I want to thank you for being such a great listener during this trip. I really appreciate it, bro."

Charlie's ears sprang up as she spoke. He tilted his head from one side to another, then barked. Neo smiled and kept driving into the darkness, careful not to hit any other vehicles on a still littered highway of abandoned cars, motorcycles, trucks, and motor homes.

She shuddered and felt a heavy sadness in her heart at the thought of all the people and families who had died that were driving and the passengers in all of those vehicles; some even transformed into creatures themselves like the ones back at the diner in Wyoming.

No looking back now. There's nothing back there anyway. Any semblance of a future in her life was clearly, emphatically forward toward North Dakota. One more state to go before meeting up with Renee and her team of scientific experts.

Her thoughts were jarred when the satellite phone wedged in the left corner of the dashboard suddenly rang, sending Charlie into another one of his barking fits. She slowed the car down and gradually came to a stop in the middle of the darkened highway. Other than the car's head-lights and the interior lights, only a full moon provided a glimmer of natural light.

"Hello?"

"Great. Your phone works," Renee said on the other end. "How are you, Neo? Please tell me you have left Los Angeles already and you're well on your way to North Dakota."

"Hi, Renee. I can't tell you how happy I am to hear your voice, and yes, we've just crossed the South Dakota state lines before you called."

"We?"

"Yes, my new best friend, Charlie. He's a cute little Scottish Terrier, I think. Anyway, I adopted him and now I'm his new owner. He's a pretty awesome dog."

"That's wonderful, Neo. I'm glad that you have a travel buddy to keep you company. I'm especially happy to know that you're still alive. We were worried about you. We tried calling you twice before and got no answer. We thought they had finally gotten to you."

"Well, the bastards did try and kill me and my dog, but I have a shotgun, a sledge hammer, and a butcher's knife with me for protection. Renee, I've killed five of them on this trip so far. That's where I met Charlie. I found him near an abandoned big rig in Nevada. His owner and his wife morphed into alien creatures, and I had to kill them, too."

"My goodness, you've been a busy young lady."

"It's been an eye opening experience to say the least, and it just keeps getting more strange and confusing," Neo said.

"I'm glad you're safe. Hopefully when you get here, we can all put our heads together and clear up some of the confusion."

"That would be wonderful."

"It should only take you another seven or eight hours to get to us from South Dakota, barring any more unforeseen life-threatening trouble you may have along the way."

"I'm excited to meet you, Renee. I've got plenty of ammo to protect myself, and Charlie is a great guard dog."

"Ammo, huh? Sounds like you've had a few wars in the trenches out there."

"More than I had anticipated, actually. I can't wait to tell you the rest of the details when I see you."

"We're looking forward to documenting all of your experiences from day one, starting with when the ooze rain first fell. We need you to stay safe and get to us in one piece so that my team can continue to gather research in an effort to figure out why all of this happened in the first place," Renee said.

"Any clues so far?"

"Not really. Unfortunately, we still have far more questions than answers. The additional information you provide will be exceedingly helpful. I'm going to hang up now, so save the juice in your battery. I will call you every three hours from this point forward until you reach our location, and I have the pleasure of seeing your smiling face in person."

"Sounds good to me, Renee, and ditto that."

"Stay safe, Neo."

"I will. I promise. I'll see you sometime tomorrow afternoon."

"Looking forward to it – bye for now."

"Bye, Renee."

After hanging up the phone, Neo sat in the car and stared out. She opened a bottle of water, took a long drink, then let out a big sigh. She looked over at Charlie and rubbed under his furry chin as he licked her hand in return. She then filled his aluminum bowl with fresh water and the dog hopped down to the floor on the passenger side and took in a long drink of his own before hopping back up on the seat.

"Won't be long now, little guy. I think this is a good spot for me to get some sleep. What's your vote?"

"Arf, arf...arf...arf!"

"Figured you say that."

***

Neo woke up the next morning to nudges against her arm and licks on her cheek from Charlie. She had slumped deep into the drivers' seat of the Mercedes, and had covered herself during the night in warm, wool blanket. Seeing the bright morning sunshine immediately lifted her spirits as she rose up and stretched out her torso, her spine crackling in response.

She let Charlie out to do his morning business, then opened a can of Little Smokies sausages to feed him breakfast. She poured out the leftover water and dumped his food into his bowl. Charlie didn't wait for her to finish emptying the can into his bowl.

"Okay, okay. Slow down, will you." She watched him quickly scarf down his meal. "Why do dogs just swallow their food when they're hungry? Try chewing it first, you'll enjoy it more."

Hungry herself, she opened a box of chocolate flavored Pop Tarts for breakfast, washing them down with bottled water. Lost in deep thought for a moment or so, by the time she looked over to check on Charlie, his bowl was empty and he was licking the sides of it.

"What are you, a magician?" she asked Charlie. "You sure made that food disappear in a hurry."

The best thing for Neo to do now was continue driving west and put as many miles behind her as she could. In front of them, the freeway lay clear and empty of life. It was nothing more than a bumper-to-bumper twisted mass of metal and plastic.

The past, where Neo lived, had been stolen away forever. The future was unknown, offering nothing more than potential and uncertainty.

20

NEO HAD ARRIVED well into the state of North Dakota. She was almost to Renee. She was so excited about having the opportunity to meet her as she grown much admiration and respect for the scientist.

The satellite phone rang again.

"Hello?"

"Hi, Neo, it's me, Renee. How much closer are you now to our facility?"

"Hi, Renee. Good to hear from you again. I figure we should be there in about forty-five minutes or so."

"Good. We'll be expecting you. You still have the detailed directions that I gave you to get us, correct?"

"I sure do. I should have no problem finding your complex. I'll call you when I'm ten minutes away to give you a heads up that I'll be there soon."

"Excellent. We'll see you then, and by the way, allow me to be the first person to say welcome to North Dakota."

"Thanks, Renee.

***

Neo kept her promise and called Renee when she was ten-minutes from the Climate Research Center complex. The weather had naturally turned much cooler now and Neo was wrapped up in a heavy, hooded winter parka and gloves.

As she drove through the complex where Renee and her team lived and worked, she was in awe of its beauty. The grounds were immaculate, nothing like the bland scenery and buildings she had imagined a science complex to look like.

As she drove up to the main building, she saw a tall, slender, attractive woman standing at the entrance. The mere sight of actually seeing another real human being live and in person brought tears to her eyes. As she pulled into a parking space in front of the building, she first had to let Charlie out to take care of his business that dogs do. It gave Renee a chance to walk toward Neo and extend her hand in greeting. What she got back was something entirely different.

"Renee!" Neo yelled out as she ran up to the scientist and proceeded to wrap her in a bear hug, squeezing her tightly as the tears flowed freely.

"I'm so glad to finally see you," Neo said as her words were muffled by Renees shoulder. Neo had pressed her face against her chest so hard, her words were barely audible as she spoke.

"It's wonderful to see you as well, Neo. I'm glad you made it here safely and in one piece."

"Me, too." Neo pulled back from her bear hug of Renee and wiped tears away with her hand.

"So this is your little hero companion, I see," Renee said, right at the moment that Charlie was pooping in the front yard of the building.

"Sorry about that, Renee," Neo said embarrassingly. "I'll clean that up, I promise."

Renee threw her head back in laughter. "Don't even worry about it, my dear. We have more important things to get started on. Charlie's poop can certainly wait until later," she said, expressing a bit of humor to help them both feel more comfortable.

"Come inside and meet my team, Charlie too, and I'll show you around."

"I can't wait. Charlie, come on boy, time to go inside." The dog came running toward them and joined the two ladies as they entered the science building. Inside, the interior was beautifully and tastefully decorated, although a bit sterile and lacking an abundance of furniture.

Neo guessed that's just the way scientists are wired. She didn't care because Renee informed her that once she got settled in and met everyone, she could retreat to her living quarters and finally shower and feel clean again.

As the two women walked through the large building, Renee filled Neo in on her plans in trying to figure what caused the ooze rain and why was it so deadly. Renee led her to the front of a brightly lit room and they stopped at the door.

Renee then flashed her badge under a identification sensor unit on the wall. Once it recognized her as being legit, it beeped three times, unlocking the double doors to the room where her colleagues were all waiting to meet Neo.

One by one she was warmly greeted by Drs. Tyler Richardson, Monica Fillmore, Jason Carter, Abby Clingensmith, Rodney Jackson, and Paul Devlin, all of them PhD scientists of various expertise. Each scientist extended their hands to greet her, but each time, Neo gave them warm hugs. The scientists also enjoying petting and playing with Charlie.

After the meet and greet, Renee informed Neo that she would now escort her to her living quarters to shower before having dinner with the scientists. The thought of taking a long hot shower, and also giving Charlie a much needed bath afterward, excited Neo.

"I'll send Monica for you in two hours. Will that give you enough time to bath, change clothes, and get settled in?"

"Two hours is plenty of time for me, Renee, and thank you. This room is gorgeous."

"You're welcome. See you and Charlie at dinner in a couple of hours, and by the way, we do have dog food on hand waiting for him."

"He'll be happy to know that, believe me."

Just being around other human beings, not just one, but several, made Neo feel whole again.

***

At dinner, Renee and her team laid their plans all out for Neo, and frankly, much of what they said surprised her, even shocked her to some extent. If the dead alien rising to feast on the living hadn't been enough, now Renee and her team had found a way to make alien creatures more civilized so they could easily live among humans.

Alien Serum Project, as Renee had called it, was a scientifically and biologically advanced project concerned with the research and development of chemical, biological, and radiological materials capable of being sprayed upon the bodies of alien creatures in an effort to control their behavior and make them more human like.

Are you kidding me? Neo was thinking while Renee continued to explain her plans. For days Neo risked her life defending herself against those grotesque looking things, and now Renee wants to civilize them? What's next, inviting them over for a casual dinner and conversation? The whole thing sounded absurd to her.

For the first time, Neo wondered if Renee and her team were a bunch mad scientists. Out of respect for the scientists, and especially Renee, whom she had grown fond of, Neo decided to keep an open mind and keep listening and asking questions. Neo was no scientist, and she certainly was no PhD, so perhaps she's missing the big picture while enjoying dinner with these remarkably intelligent scientists.

The University of North Dakota Climate Research Center was the primary test site for the blood serum, led by Renee. It was a covert alien research operation experimenting in extraterrestrial mind control. Renee wanted her team, along with Neo and Charlie, to blanket the alien creatures with serum spray, then capture them for interrogation and to extract information about their species and existence.

Very creepy.

Essentially, the aliens would serve as guinea pigs for scientific and biological research purposes.

***

Trying to recall any of the long explanation from Renee as to why the scientific team had plans for Charlie to risk his neck as bait and draw as many alien creatures into a trap and then hose them down with blood serum, then capture and interrogate them made Neo's head spin.

Mad scientists, indeed. She was convinced of it now.

Renee compiled research which tracked other species of alien creatures over a long-term. She tells Neo that aliens had normally traveled in packs ten years ago. She had reported the findings to the university and finally, two weeks before the ooze rain came crashing down, a department head shot the idea down.

Renee gave Neo a needle containing a sample of the serum. It consisted of a clear, pale-yellow liquid. Her orders were simple: find the largest group of alien creatures and expose their skin to the blood serum. Renee had estimated that the best way to do that, and keep her team at arms length and safe from the vicious, deadly aliens, was to hose them down in a downpour of blood serum.

Neo didn't like that idea at all. She wanted to kill all of them, not preserve and study them. Renee and her team had obviously assumed that she would go along with their bizarre plans. She felt pressured to agree with everything and willingly participate in a soon to be alien witch hunt.

This was *not* what Neo had expected to hear. She drove over two thousand miles for this? What could she do otherwise? If she rejected Renee's plans and decided to opt out of actively participating in hunting aliens, what would their reaction be? Would they kick her out of the facility? If they did, where would she go? She was too far away from home to drive back to Los Angeles, or just tell Renee *no, thanks,* grab Charlie, get in the car and keep driving to *nowhere.*

Neo decided to speak up. She told Renee and her team how she felt about their plans and offered alternative plan consisting of *let's just kill the bastards.* Renee and her team shot that idea down quickly. Neo was outnumbered, out-manned, and now stuck with a bunch of weirdo scientists with nowhere else to go. Great, just great.

Renee suggested that Neo sleep on the idea of her blood serum plan, and wake up the next morning with a clearer mind. Neo agreed.

After an hour of tossing and turning, she was finally able to fall asleep with Charlie already knocked out on the bed at Neo's feet.

The next morning and after much deliberation, Neo decided to go with the flow and see how things go. Perhaps Renee and her team knew something that Neo didn't, and the alien creatures would serve as valuable tools of information in discovering why the ooze rain fell and how the virus, the dust, and the mutated aliens are deeply intertwined.

Plus, she had no idea she would ever again come in contact with other human beings if she left the comfortable confines and amenities of the science facility. Even if she were now living among wierdo scientists, they were still human. She figured she had experience in killing a few of them which gave her confidence for this undertaking.

When it was all said and done after again conversing with Renee and her team, it was either get on board one-hundred percent with the Alien Serum Project, or get on the road again with Charlie to nowhere, and a life of isolation and most likely more powerful, stronger, alien killers.

With that in mind, it seemed an easy, yet reluctant choice for Neo.

***

Venturing outside to hunt for aliens was risky when they were running around with the ability to kill a person instantly.

Neo was quick and fast and she hustled until she laid in wait and came in contact with a group of six creatures five miles outside of Grand Forks, just off the highway. She nearly threw the canister of blood serum down and drew her shotgun on them, but she didn't.

She waited until one of the alien creatures came within ten feet of her hiding place, then began blasting it with it with blood serum. The large canisters had the capability of shooting serum up to twenty-five feet away.

Renee had told her that the serum would take biological effect within their alien systems in 24-hours, rendering them defenseless and essentially short-term paralyzed, much like wild animals are shot with a tranquilizer gun to temporarily immobilize them so that they may be tagged and their movements tracked. It's the same concept Renee had in mind all along.

Why are Charlie and I doing all the work? Why isn't Renee or any of the other very capable scientists out here helping me spray these slimy freaks?

Neo could come up with only one answer: Just as the alien creatures are now guinea pigs, so to is she. Renee needed her and Charlie to do the *front end* dirty work while the others sit in their comfortable facility and pour over data and information once the aliens are captured.

Actually, it's Dr. Tyler Richardson and Dr. Rodney Jackson's job on the *back end* to drive their four-wheel gator to the locations Neo gives them, and pick up the creatures to bring them back to a sealed off, jail-like area below the main floor of the facility for further observation.

She circled circled the remaining tribe of aliens, spraying them all. Then the oddest thing happened. The group of aliens turned and shuffled away in a disorderly manner. Neo shook herself out of her stance. She felt dull, like a knife that had been used too many times.

Bones in the alien's faces were thinner and more fragile than any others she had previously seen. She always knew that if a particular alien had enough intelligence it could destroy her face to unrecognizable proportions, lifting it right off her skull.

She hadn't informed Renee that in addition to bringing Charlie and the bag of serum canisters with her, she also brought along her fully loaded shotgun. Deep inside, she hated those things, and for good reason. Neo scooped up a canister and drew her shotgun. A pack of aliens was just up the highway meandering around.

"Hey!" she yelled out to them. They all quickly turned with the exact same expressionless look on their morbid faces. She walked up to them and had gotten within ten feet before she started spraying them. She noticed one of them had red-tipped fingers and shot it in the head.

"What was that?" Renee said over the hand-held portable radio. "Dammit, Neo. I said not to destroy any of them."

"Sorry, Renee. I thought one of them was going to take my head off. It got too close."

"Remember, Neo, our first order of business is to pursue and recover. Now finish up and get back here as soon as you can," Renee said.

"10-4"

Neo scowled, and wondered what had happened to the kind, sweet, thoughtful, caring Renee she knew not so long ago?

Another group of aliens that she found reacted the same way as the last group when she finished a canister. They turned and headed in the direction they had been going before she arrived. It seemed that the blood serum was also an alien repellent?

Much later, after Neo decided she wasn't in a hurry to get back to the facility, Renee checked in with her again.

"How are things going out there, Neo?"

"Okay, I guess. I'm watching a pack of alien creatures, waiting for them to get a bit closer."

"Can you make it back to the facility?"

"Uh, that's a negative, Renee."

"You said you are in a pack. Just to be specific— are you in a pack of aliens?"

"That's affirmative."

"Neo, tell me, have you noticed any altered behaviors in them?" There was patch of static and when it cleared Neo was saying, "— over on the hill. They've been following me."

"I'm sorry, Neo, I lost you for a moment. Who's following you?"

"Another group of aliens. At first they retracted when I sprayed them. Now it seems as if they're somehow attracted to the serum."

"That's very interesting. Do they still smell like strong ammonia?"

"Unfortunately, yes. What's that got to do with anything?"

"Well, the serum should eliminate their putrid order almost instantly so that when Dr. Richardson and Dr. Jackson pick them up in the morning and bring them back, our facility won't become unbearable to live in."

"So somebody else is spraying them? Some other group of scientists?" Neo asked.

"No," Renee said. "Not possible. We're the only facility capable of any such thing for at least a hundred mile radius.

Any scientific group wouldn't have ventured this far to experiment. The danger from traveling all the way here and traveling all the way back to their lab to monitor their subjects would have been too great."

"What?" Neo said, not quite understanding all of Renee's scientist lingo.

"Previously, we began our own experiment. If the ooze rain were any other natural phenomena, I imagine it would have manifested well before now. There is no legitimate explanation for this, Neo. There is no 'something else' unless someone has some factor none of our dwindling scientific community has considered, which I doubt."

***

When Neo felt stubborn enough she moved fast. At seven the next morning she was in the arsenal, zipping up a duffel bag full of weapons. She didn't care what Renee said, she wasn't going to spend another night tracking aliens with Charlie with only canisters of blood serum to protect herself with. Strangely, despite all the serum laden aliens that were being brought back to the facility, they didn't seem to be eating people anymore.

On this night, Renee decided to tag along with Neo to make sure she was doing her job to the very best of her ability. Then Neo purposely ran off and left Renee all alone. Furious, Renee contacted her on the hand-held radio.

"Neo, where are you?"

"I'm just going to see if anything is around."

"Neo, get back here. I'm all alone."

"I'll be right back, Renee. Don't worry."

All along, Neo wasn't watching aliens. She was watching Renee from not too far away.

Renee could feel eyes on her. A few more feet and she would be clear.

"Renee! It was Renee!"

Dammit.

Neo took off running and a moment later heard a bullet whiz off somewhere in the distance. She rounded the corner and was clear momentarily. Her camo was bright enough to make out in the weak moonlight, but she gambled that if she got at least fifty yards away Renee wouldn't pursue her.

There was no turning back now. If Renee and her team of mad scientists wouldn't have killed her before, they certainly would now. She was as dead as if a alien creature was chomping on her arm. Renee had purposely created a group of alien creatures that have the mental capacity to problem solve. That made them potentially unstoppable and extremely dangerous.

***

For the first time since she encountered the baby monster above her apartment, Neo couldn't remember the last time she had seen a child. The latest group of aliens contained one, who happened to walk up on her unexpectedly.

She holstered her shotgun to her chest and pushed the girl back by the shoulders to get a better look at her. She was filthy and smelled awful. Her tangled black hair was a mess that had grown to her knees. She was pretty. Perhaps not traditionally so, but in that all children are beautiful. Neo surprised even herself by showing no fear. She couldn't understand why. The young girl was looking down when Neo hooked her finger under her chin and raised her face.

"Are you okay, honey," she asked the girl. Her shale grey eyes flashed up and Neo knew something was wrong. There wasn't any time to stop it as the little girl opened her mouth and sprayed a putrid yellow fluid all over the front of Neo's T-shirt.

Neo reared back and nearly fell on her ass. She pulled her shotgun out of its holster and fired where she thought the girl was, hoping she could at least wound the thing before it could attack her at some later point. She dug out her bottle of water from her thigh pocket and rinsed herself with water to clean the ooze off of her T-shirt.

The little girl was gone. Perhaps that ooze the girl spewed was meant to debilitate her. She was okay, but that could change at any moment. Wherever the little girl had scampered off to, she was quick. Other than a few abandoned vehicles spread out from each other, there wasn't anything else to hide behind.

The smelly, yellow ooze had no other effect on Neo. If it wasn't poison, then what the hell was it?

The sky had turned crimson by the time she saw another alien moving about. It was old, with black skin and its eyes were filmed over like a snake. Its forearm was broken and half its hand was missing. It had no legs, but it propped itself up on its hips.

Is this what Renee has been breeding for so long. Speaking of Renee, who had taken off on foot earlier, came running up to Neo in fear.

"You have to get me outta here," she begged, banging on the fence Neo was leaning against.

"No, Renee." Neo's tone was calm. "You need to do one of two things: get yourself out, or survive the night alive. You created this, you deal with it."

Suddenly, an alien attacked Neo and Renee unexpectedly. Neo raised her shotgun and pulled the trigger. The gunshot jerked the alien erect again and it looked up to see Neo standing above it. The creature's eyes were half-lidded and it was dead before its ass had hit the ground.

Neo then rushed at the alien, pulled her butcher's knife from the leather holster strapped to her left leg and sliced off one of its tentacles. Another creature grabbed her shoulder and she spun and sliced off its tentacle.

A third alien lunged at her and her blade sliced through it head and eyes, blinding it. Her shoulder bumped the last creature and Neo was about to bring both her machetes down on its head when she noticed that it was *Renee*.

She hesitated and stared into Renee's eyes. Neo knew it was no longer the friend she had trusted. Renee was a full-fledged alien creature now, just like the others. Neo halted her wide swing of the knife away from Renee.

"Renee, I don't want to do this. Please don't make me do this." Renee didn't stop coming toward her. Neo took a swing at her arm and she almost ripped one of Renee's tentacles off.

"I'm for real this time, Renee. Don't make me do it!"

"Neo. It's me." Her voice was a whisper.

There was a moment of silence between the two friends, until reality set in.

"Sorry, Renee. You're not what you used to be."

Neo chopped into Renee's head and her knife made it midway down her forehead before the alien that used to be her human friend slumped to the ground, quivering. Her friend was barely recognizable – a soulless, corpse-like version of her former self.

When Renee's gruesome head and tentacles stopped twitching, Neo covered her mouth and resisted the urge to vomit. She then realized why she hesitated killing her. It had been in her eyes. Despite Renee coming at her, despite her dirt-covered growling teeth, despite the huge gash in her head, she could tell Renee didn't want to do what she was doing. Perhaps she offered herself to be killed in order to save mankind and reverse the evil that she had done.

Neo turned to walk in the other direction when she spotted the same little alien girl she had seen before. The girl was standing about thirty feet away in between two abandoned pickup trucks. Neo knew that this time she had to kill the girl or whoever she used to be, or it would kill her.

She started to walk toward the girl with the knife in one hand and her shotgun in the other. When they were ten feet apart, the little girl began to walk toward her. Neo gripped the handle of the knife tighter. At five feet apart the girl suddenly dipped and dashed inside one of the rusty old abandoned trucks.

Neo kept walking toward her.

When she got to the truck, Neo swung the door open, but she didn't see the little girl, who had exited from the other side. Out of nowhere, the girl skittered over the roof of the truck, grunted and lunged at her. There wasn't much clearance as the other truck was at Neo's back.

Neo jerked the knife backward and twice swung it at the girl's head with authority. The girl leaned back effortlessly causing two loud *swoosh* sounds as Neo missed its head both times. The girl swung her sharp right tentacle down toward Neo's head, who ducked just in time to avoid her own head being cut right down the middle. Neo staggered back. The girl watched her, her head cocked to the side.

By the time Neo was able to move again, the girl began to swing both tentacles wildly at her. Neo grunted. The alien girl grunted back at her. Suddenly, the little girl began laughing at her. It was enjoying this battle.

Confused, Neo looked up at the girl still perched atop the truck. She squinted her eyes and shook her head to regain her composure before lifting her arm and taking another forceful swing at the girl's head, who ducked again with ease.

The girl then grunted. What was odd is that Neo felt as if she understood what the alien girl was trying to communicate to her. Neo raised her arm again, but not before the girl grunted once more. No, the little girl was saying. How? She hadn't actually *said* it.

The alien girl creature grunted yet again. *Come with me,* it sounded like.

Neo should have killed her right then and there, but she froze in amazement. She lowered the knife in her hand and stared at the girl's mouth, whose tongue played over the lining of its gums in its mouth. Her gums were red and badly swollen, throbbed, and pulsed until they had bulged out.

The female alien creature had succeeded in catching Neo off guard and took advantage of her temporary relaxed state, and pounced on her from above. Neo quickly raised her arm still holding the butcher's knife, and the girl's body landed on the blade.

Neo lowered its quivering body to the ground. To be on the safe side, she stabbed the thing several more times, recognizing the all too familiar stench of ammonia and yellow ooze leaking from its body. That was no helpless little girl. That thing was a monster in disguise, another predator, created by Renee, that Neo had not seen before which answers to why she seemed so confused.

***

It groaned but stood. Neo whirled and squeezed the trigger on the shotgun, but it clicked empty. "Shit! Not again!" It was the second time her shotgun had jammed, perhaps from overuse. She racked the shaft and began to fire away, but the alien was gone. The shotgun was now empty of rounds. Neo then fled back into the science building to get more ammunition.

Neo threw the doors of the building open and pounded up the stairs. She tried to locate more shotgun shells before the place becomes overrun with aliens. With Renee dead, they no longer had a leader of the pack who put major restrictions or boundaries on them. They could now do what they wanted to do without recourse. It was now a *free-for-all.*

Neo knew that sooner rather than later the creatures would be getting closer to overtaking the science facility, and there were more of them now. *Gee, thanks a lot, Renee,* she thought. She was able to get to her stash of shotgun shells and loaded up, and then some. She suddenly turned to head downstairs when she was shocked to see that a creature was standing ten feet away from her. That didn't take long.

"You could have at lease knocked before entering the room," Neo sarcastically said to the creature. It took a step forward and reached for her no more than five feet away. She squeezed the trigger of her shotgun and its head exploded.

Neo looked up and saw that there were other alien creatures not too far behind it and she started running. The other aliens rushed over and pushed their alien brethren aside as Neo turned around to see how close they were to her as she racked the shotgun and fired right into the chest of the next one.

It didn't die like the others, but struggled against the blast, managing to knock two other aliens down just behind it. She racked again and took another one's head off before racking and turning back to the stairs. She was almost to the fifth floor when she could feel them close behind her again. There must have been eight to ten of them.

She turned and pumped three rounds into the surging crowd. The mob of alien creatures had to climb over the litter of bodies in her wake, and she served up the first two a few head shots apiece before her shotgun emptied again.

Neo pulled spare ammo from her chest holster and reloaded while she ran. She brushed against something on her belt loop that she had forgotten about. It was a hand grenade that she grabbed from the facility weapons room in the basement. She squeezed it as if she didn't believe it was real as she had never operated one before. She had to use it correctly and soon. The aliens were too close to not get this right.

She pulled the pin on the grenade, spun around at the top of the stairs and rolled it down, listening to it clank as it bounced step-by-step. She then counted to three before throwing herself to the next flight of stairs, clapping her hands over her ears.

Boom!

The walls shook. She hoped she didn't also bring the entire building down on her head. Neo didn't plan on being inside when the building came down anyway. She took a second to look back, barely able to see the bottom flight of stairs had disappeared behind a huge cloud of smoke, along with all of the aliens that had wanted to kill her.

Neo was now able to catch her breath and climb a bit slower up the steps to the top.

At the top, she swung the door open then dropped and rolled onto the roof. When she stood, the awful smell of ammonia was almost as bad up here as it was on the stairs. To her right were two large HVAC units. Something grunted not too far behind her.

She had to hurry.

Two aliens appeared out of nowhere, wrapping their tentacles around her ankles, causing her to stumble and fall. Her hearing had to have been blunted by the grenade blast because she sure as hell didn't hear more of them coming after her again.

Neo squeezed the shotgun trigger and the first one flew backward violently, after she blasted several rounds into its torso. She then pulled the knife out of her leg holster and sliced off its dangling tentacle, tossed it up in the air, and with her right leg, punted it across the rooftop like a football.

A second alien creature reached out a tentacle and grabbed her right ankle. With the knife in her right hand, she leaned down and stabbed at where she guessed its face was. It wailed and quickly released her ankle. The six-foot-tall alien roared at Neo, and she responded with two shotgun blasts to its forehead.

"*Never* grope a lady without her permission."

Does this get any easier, she thought, not factoring in the fiasco from the stairs. She walked over to where she thought the two aliens had come from to make sure more of them hadn't arrived late to the party. Neo glanced across to the next building over. What remained of it after the grenade explosion, was still two stories higher, and much too far for her to jump.

Neo saw something move out of the corner of her eye to her right. She looked down and eyeballed yet another alien creature quickly closing in on her. This time she heard it shuffling across the floor of the roof.

"What took you so long? You're late to my party."

The creature locked eyes with her. She could see the recognition in its eyes. It was spooky, as if it was still partially human in some way, and likely was. Was it one of Renee's scientist team members? It certainly looked male to her. Its stare held all the factors of a living human being who had been cornered and knew he was about to die.

It roared and lunged at her. Neo blasted its head off.

The rooftop's foundation suddenly shifted. A huge crunching sound followed. She had to throw her arms out to catch her balance and keep from falling as the building had pitched to an angle. What remained of the foundations was going to give all the way soon. Neo slipped the shotgun into its shouldered holster and swung her legs down a nearby ladder.

The building was teetering on complete collapse by the time she got to the bottom. She stepped over the bodies of several dead alien creatures as she heard a tremendous snap. However, instead of a collapse, it seemed more like the building was lying down to sleep as it shifted in slow motion. All the walls folded in, trapping and crushing anything inside.

Neo could hear other aliens moaning and crying out for help inside. Safely off the ladder on standing on solid ground again, she hurried back to the Mercedes when she spotted a badly injured alien creature bleeding yellow ooze and limping across the ground. Its tentacles were nearly broken in two, and one of its legs was twisted awkwardly.

Neo shot the thing in the head before it even laid eyes on her.

She finally reached the car, opened the door, and cautiously searched inside for an alien hiding in wait. Her eyes grew as large as a dinner plate when she saw something furry, panting, with a wet nose and a wagging tail crawl out from under the passenger side seat.

"Charlie! You made it! You're alive!"

She hugged her dog, and she hopped into the car, started the engine, and peeled away.

Neo held her breath and suddenly slammed on the brakes. Up ahead about fifty feet was a swarm of aliens in the road. Their tentacles waved in the air as they ran toward her.

"How many more of these things did Renee breed?"

She threw the car into reverse. The creatures were running now and spitting. She revved the engine and the Mercedes rolled backwards, but not fast enough. Soon they were upon her. One of the creatures swung and ripped off the driver's side mirror. Another whipped its tentacles at the window in an attempt to break it, with no luck. Other aliens flanked the passenger's side and banged on the roof and window, causing Charlie to bark his head off again.

"Back off, you damn freaks!" Neo shouted at them as she swerved the wheel to break away from them. She felt the tires run over a pair of tentacles and yellow ooze shooting high in the air, and saw one of the aliens tumble over.

She slammed on the brakes, bringing the Mercedes to a halt, then quickly threw the transmission into drive. The creatures continued to pound on the windows as she stabbed her foot into the gas pedal and sped forward, sending a couple of them flying off from the car roof.

Neo now wanted to use the Mercedes as a lethal weapon. She aimed the car at a group of aliens ready to pounce on the car. They hissed, raised their sharp tentacles in anger, and prepared themselves to jump toward the car.

"Yeah, that's right! Keep coming!"

She plowed into about five of them like a 4,000 pound bowling ball, hurling them over the hood of the Mercedes and back onto the road. Another had fallen behind and collapsed, apparently injured. Even with the windows rolled all the way up, she could still smell the foul odor of ammonia, blood, and decay that found its way through the vents.

Neo sat quietly in the car for a moment to catch her breath after this round of aliens were killed. She knew there likely were more to com. Her satellite phone rang. She felt her heart skip a beat. She answered it.

"Hello?"

A voice resonated from the other end. It was Dr. Tyler Richardson, one of Renee's scientists.

"Neo! It's me, Dr. Richardson. Are you okay?"

"Yeah, I'm good, Charlie is, too. We just killed a few more of those things. You sound human, but how do I know you're not one of those clever, advanced aliens that can make his voice sound like another person?"

"I'm certainly no alien, that's for sure. Renee hadn't got to that point yet of transforming their voice boxes from growling creature to articulate human, and thank God, but she was certainly working on it."

"Why did Renee do it, Dr. Richardson? Why?"

"Renee was a great scientist and a good person. She was blessed with one of the most innovative scientific minds ever," Dr. Richardson said. "However, Renee also had a far more sinister and selfish side that twisted her mind. It caused her experiment to later go terribly, terribly wrong."

"The more you talk, doctor, the more I'll believe this is really you. Keep talking."

"Certainly, I understand. In spite of her enormous gifts and talents as a world-renown scientist and researcher, Renee was also the Frankenstein of our modern times. She was fascinated by the idea that an alien, much like the caveman had evolved into an intelligent being over centuries, could be morphed into a smart, articulate, problem solving species in a short period of time, effectively eliminating having to wait decades for the process to come to fruition."

"And you and the others just went along with it?"

"No. None of us wanted to participate in the experiment. We knew it was wrong. However we were all employed by the University of North Dakota Climate Research Center project not long after the NASA accident. We had to go along with it as our careers, any later advancement, and our livliehood depended on it. We have few other options. It was either stay on board, or quit."

"The NASA accident? What do you mean? What happened?"

"Through her vast connections with top-level personnel at NASA, and using the university science center as her backdrop, Renee was able to stow away one of her deadly virus raging, smaller-sized mutated aliens during the Gemini9 space shuttle mission launch in 2008."

"Was it a successful mission for NASA? What ever happened to the alien?"

"The launch itself was a great success, sending the space shuttle millions of miles into outer space. During a routine inventory check, one of the crew shuttle astronauts discovered the container that housed the alien. It was empty. They knew something was wrong and a shuttle cabin search began. The creature found them before they found it, killing all six astronauts.

"The alien then, as it was programmed to do, blew it self to pieces, along with the space shuttle, sending massive amounts of killer virus particles into the atmosphere, which ultimately severely altered its intricate climate control system.

"Five years later, here comes the highly infected ooze rain, which in turn infected people who came in contact with it, killing them and wiping out civilization as we know it, only to eventually be replaced worldwide by Renee's intelligent species of aliens who could breed, and its females, reproduce."

"Oh, my, God. I can't believe this. I touched some of the ooze rain by accident, and a bit of the dust that came afterward. It didn't infect me. Any explanation as to why, doctor?"

"Believe it, Neo. It's all true. The government hushed the details of the obliteration of the space shuttle, choosing to not report any evidence that there was a lethal virus released which could eventually trickle down into our atmosphere at a later point, and it certainly did.

"The dust was simply a byproduct of the ooze. It's the dried flakes of skin from the contaminated particles that floated around the air for a few days seeking to reconnect back to the skin of its owner, the ooze itself. Neo, do you know your blood type?"

"So that's where the ooze rain and dust came from. Now I know. It's been a long time since I had to think about my blood type, but I believe it's type O, why?"

"Then it makes sense. You see, type O blood has neither A nor B antigens in its red cells. Both of your A and B antibodies are in your plasma. What it means is that you're immune to all but the more advanced killer alien creatures. Thus the reason why you were repeatedly ignored. You're essentially a living, walking, talking, alien repellant, for the most part."

"I guess I just wasn't good enough for them, I suppose."

"Correct, you aren't, except for the advanced aliens. They're the ones you definitely want to avoid at all costs."

"Well, I made it this far, right?"

"Yes, you certainly have and I applaud you. Since all the aliens were created with human-like bodies and internal organs, they *can* be killed, but once an advanced alien latches on to you, if you don't kill it first, it will surely kill you, so continue to be careful."

"I'll be careful, I promise, and thank you for heads up."

Neo's mind drifted back to her former friend, Renee.

"Renee seemed like one of the good guys, you know?"

"She was, at least for the first ten years of her career here at the Climate Center. Neo, scientific minds such as Renee's oftentimes believe that the evils that they're performing are actually doing good in the world. That's what made her a mad scientist, if you will."

"So what happens to you and the other scientists now. Where do you all go from here?"

"I'm the last one left. The others were killed by the alien creatures shortly after Renee died. I just happened to be the lucky one and I barricaded myself in my quarters and rode out the killings. It was awful. I could hear them being slaughtered one-by-one. Neo, you have to help me stop them. I know a way to destroy all of the rest of them, including the advanced stage aliens, and there are many, many more here, but we need to..."

"Hello? Dr. Richardson. Are you there? Hello?"

Neo could hear a sudden crash through the phone, as if numerous aliens had found Dr. Richardson and broke through his barricade. She heard him scream in agony several times as she listened to the sounds of the aliens killing him, likely ripping him to shreds. To his credit, it also sounded like he fought them with all his might before they killed him.

She stood frozen in place, the phone still in her hand and up to her ear. When the horrible sounds finally subsided after a few minutes, she could breathing on the other end. Was it Dr. Richardson? Perhaps he had somehow survived the attack and need to give her one more piece of pertinent information to assist in her future survival.

Instead of the doctor, she heard the familiar deep groans of an alien. When it spoke to her, yes, spoke to her in a slow, deep, gravely voice. It was by no means articulate, but Neo heard what it said clear as day. It sent a massive shudder throughout her body.

"Join...us."

She quickly hung up and ended the call.

***

So far the highways were clear of aliens as Neo had left the science facility for good, and continued driving north. Thirsty, she reached between the seats for a bottle of water she had stored there. She threw her head back and took a long drink from it.

"Your turn, Charlie," she said. "You gotta be thirsty by now, too." She pulled to a stop in the middle of the road and poured the remaining water into his doggy bowl. Charlie hopped down from the passenger seat and lapped the water up until it was all gone.

"Good boy."

As the two friends sat and exhaled, taking advantage of a rare quiet moment as the sun had begun to set, a strange thing happened. Just as Dr. Richardson had said when they first met, it began to rain. It wasn't normal rain drops that were coming down. One by one, more rain drops fell from the sky and more heavily.

Neo instantly recognized the type of rain. It was ooze rain. Not more than a week earlier, the same type of gooey, yellow-red ooze rain began pummeling everything in sight on the streets in Los Angeles.

She turned on the car's windshield wipers to get a better view of it outside. When the wipers made contact with the ooze rain particles, instead of quickly wiping them away like normal rain drop, the ooze rain made it seem like the wipers were smearing thick chucks of ketchup all over the windshield, obscuring the view.

What she saw moments later made her jaw drop and her eyes grow wider.

Alien creatures, lots of them, began uprooting from the ground along each side of the highway. It was as if the dead were rising from their graves. Through the ooze rain, Neo could see each and every alien extending their tentacles toward the sky and waving them around as if they were trying to catch each glob of ooze onto their tentacles like a child with a butterfly net trying to catch a butterfly.

Alien life had abused Earth for more than a week, killing people, and the environment, which had to reluctantly succumb to the violence of the ooze rain. This time however, instead of killing entire populations of humans, the ooze rain gradually killed all alien kind. It was as if Earth had its fill of death and destruction, and today was payback time.

She heard the aliens groaning in unison. One by one, she watched them drop to the ground like the dead weight that they were about to become, or had already been. It was as if someone reached behind and unplugged them, along with their past; ending one chapter, perhaps to begin a better one.

Within minutes, each and every alien literally evaporated into the chilly, thin North Dakota air, only to seconds later turn into dust. This time the dust settled, serving as a final resting place for the evil that it used to be, in the mutated body that served as its cover.

Nothing was ever normal again.

"Time to go, Charlie boy, to...*nowhere.*"

"You know something Charlie, maybe somewhere out there, there's a really cute guy with type O blood who survived like I did, waiting for me, who's *not* an alien. It's all up to me now. I'm the last female alive with the ability to reproduce and begin a new civilization. I'm only twenty-seven, still young enough to start a family some day,which I've always wanted to do but was always too busy to do anything about it."

During the past week, Neo had thought about what it would be like to have a normal life again. Maybe she would've gone to college for her PhD and majored in Biology, or History, or perhaps even met the man of her dreams.

Who knows what lies ahead.

It's not good to dwell in the past, her father would say, but sometimes, the past is all you have.

DAVID BROWN

The Most Entertaining Author in the World™

Writing *OOZE* was yet another fascinatingly enjoyable experience! I'm glad Neo and Charlie made it out of there alive. I hope you enjoyed reading their story. My fourth novel, *BIG LIFE*, is scheduled to be released March, 2014. Thank you, and remember – we're all in this together. Keep in touch at ParkwayPress.com for future excerpts, release details, and updates for *BIG LIFE*.

Best wishes,
Author David Brown